THE VIADUCT MURDER

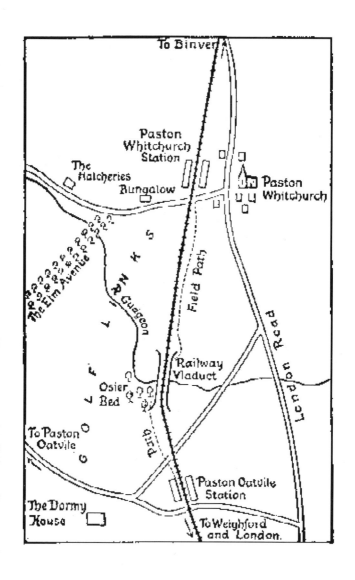

To Binver

Paston Whitchurch Station

The Hatcheries

Bungalow

Paston Whitchurch

The Elm Avenue

L I N K S

R. Gudgeon

Field Path

London Road

Railway Viaduct

G O L F

Osier Bed

Path

To Paston Oatvile

Paston Oatvile Station

The Dormy House

To Weighford and London.

LONDON — BINVER
TRAIN SCHEDULE

LONDON	3.00	3.47	..
Weighford	3.31	4.29	..
Paston Oatvile (arr.) ..	..	4.43	..
Paston Oatvile (dep.) ..	..	..	4.50
Paston Whitchurch	..	..	4.58
BINVER	3.59	..	5.09

THE
VIADUCT
MURDER

By

RONALD A. KNOX

The Merion Press
P.O. Box 144
Merion Station, PA 19066-0144
(610) 617-8919
www.merionpress.com

© **The Merion Press, 2001**
P.O. Box 144
Merion Station, PA 19066-0144

Cover by Noel G. Miles, AWS

ISBN 0-9677143-1-1

This edition first published in the year 2001
Set in Times New Roman

Printed in the United States of America

Introduction to this Edition

Someone must have already said that reading a good book is like drinking fine wine. The experience is heightened even more by its vision and bouquet. *The Viaduct Murder* meets the sight, smell, and feel good test. Witty, clever, and entertaining, it is thoroughly delightful.

Born in Leicestershire, England, on February 17, 1888, to an Anglican family, Ronald (Arbuthnott) Knox was a fascinating person. Educated at Eton and Oxford, he was appointed chaplain of Trinity College, Oxford, in 1912 and converted to Catholicism in 1917. At the same time that he served as Roman Catholic chaplain of Oxford University (1926-1939) and as domestic prelate to the Pope (1936), he wrote classic detective stories.

According to his niece, Penelope Fitzgerald, a fine author in her own right, Msgr. Knox was probably the best known Roman Catholic Bishop of his day. He single-handedly translated the St. Jerome Latin Vulgate Bible into English. His works on religious themes include: *Some Loose Stones* (1913), *Reunion All Round* (1914), *The Spiritual Aeneid* (1918), *The Belief of Catholics* (1927), *Caliban in Grub Street* (1930), *Heaven and Charing Cross* (1935), *Let Dons Delight* (1939), and *Captive Flames* (1940).

Msgr. Knox's Roman Catholicism caused his father to cut him out of his will. This did not make much difference, however, as Knox earned a good income from his detective novels. His mystery stories include: *The Viaduct Murder* (1925), *The Body in the Silo* (1933), and *Still Dead* (1934).

His niece reports that Prime Minister Harold Macmillan, an old friend of Father Knox, took him to the train station as he was dying. When Macmillan wished him a comfortable journey, Father Knox replied, "it will be a long one." He died in Somerset, England on August 24, 1957.

By way of background for this book, it is helpful to know about the early passenger trains in Great Britain. There were three classes of accommodation: First-class (highest fare), originally like a stagecoach, became an enclosed compartment with plenty of legroom, comfort, and spacious seats. It had the smoothest ride as it was farthest from the wheels. Second-class (lower fare) originally an open wagon with seats, was also later enclosed, but was simpler than first-class, and had less legroom. Third-class (lowest fare) originally had no seats — passengers had to stand or sit on the floor — became a compartment with basic fixtures and the least roominess and only basic fixtures. It had the bumpiest and noisiest ride, as it was located right over the wheels. In this book, reference is made

ii

only to "first" and "third" as second-class had completely disappeared from trains in Britain because there was little distinction between it and either of the others.

The profound influence of Conan Doyle's *Sherlock Holmes* on detective fiction can be seen throughout this work. There are no less than ten references to Holmes and/or Watson including the title of one of the chapters. It is not surprising then that Knox's *Essays in Satire* (1928) contains "Studies in the Literature of Sherlock Holmes."

THE MERION PRESS

Glossary
(page reference is to first appearance)

Dormy-house (p. 1): clubhouse; "dormie" (or dormy) in golf means being ahead by as many holes as remain to be played.

Dower-house (p. 2): widow's house.

Glebe (p. 1): land belonging or yielding revenue to a parish church.

Jeu de mots (p. 40): play on words; pun

Mattins (or matins) (p. 206): the morning prayer, which is the lengthiest of the Canonical hours. Its origin is still in dispute. The term "matins" (*matutini*) originally designated the morning hour.

Niblick (p. 1): a golf club equivalent to today's nine iron. In the era of 1900 to 1930 golf clubs were wooden shafted and balls were mesh-patterned.

Orisons (p. 188): prayers

Osier (p. 16): willow used in making furniture and basketry

CONTENTS

CONTENTS (cont'd)

CHAPTER I

THE PASTON OATVILE DORMY-HOUSE

NOTHING is ever wasted. The death of the animal fertilizes the vegetable world; bees swarm in the disused pillar-bog; sooner or later, somebody will find a use for the munition-factories. And the old country-seats of feudal England, that bask among their figured terraces, frowning at the ignoble tourist down secular avenues and thrusting back the high-road he travels by into respectful detours—these too, although the family have long since decided that it is too expensive to live there, and the agents smile at the idea of letting them like one humouring a child, have their place in the hero-tenanted England of to-day. The house itself may be condemned to the scrap-heap, but you can always make a golf-course out of the Park. Acres, that for centuries have scorned the weight of the plough, have their stubborn glebe broken with the niblick, and overpopulated greens recall the softness and the trimness of earlier lawns. Ghosts of an earlier day will walk there, perhaps, but you can always play through them.

Paston Oatvile (distrust the author whose second paragraph docs not come to ground in the particular) seemed to have been specially adapted by an inscrutable Providence for such a niche in the scheme of things. The huge Italianate building which the fifteenth Lord Oatvile raised as a monument to his greatness (he sold judiciously early out of the South Sea Company) took fire in the nineties of last century and burned for a whole night; the help given by the local fire brigade was energetic rather than considerate, and Achelous completed the havoc which Vulcan had begun. It stands even now, an indecent skeleton, papered rooms and carved mantelpieces confronting you shamefacedly, like the inside of a doll's house whose curtain-wall has swung back on the hinge. What secrets that ball-room, those powder-closets must have witnessed in the days of an earlier gallantry, when the stuccoed facade still performed its discreet office! Poor rooms, they will never know any more secrets now. The garden, too, became involved in the contagion of decay: weeds have overgrown its paved walks, and neglected balustrades have crumbled; a few of the hardier flowers still spring there, but half-smothered in rank grass, shabby-genteel survivors of an *ancien régime*. For the family never attempted to rebuild; they prudently retired to the old Manor at the other end of the park, a little brick and timber paradise which had served the family for a century and a half as dower-house. In time, even this reduced splendour was judged too expensive, and the family sold.

No need, then, to mourn for Paston Oatvile;

the sanctities of its manorial soil will be as interminable as golf. An enterprising club, seconded by an accommodating railway, has invested its rural solitude with an air of suburbanity; it is only an hour's journey from London, and the distance could be covered in three-quarters of the time if the club were less exclusive. Bungalows, each fitted with its own garage, and cottages that contain billiard-rooms have sprung up in the neighbourhood; thirty or forty of these, all rough-cast and red tiles, conceal by a series of ingenious dissimilarities their indebtedness to the brain of a single architect. In the middle of these—the cathedral, the town hall, the market-place around which all their activities centre—stands the dower-house of the Oatviles, the dormy-house of to-day. The committee have built on to it largely in what is understood to be the same style, and indeed, the new part is undeniably brick and timber, though in wet weather the timber is apt to warp and fall off. It is not only a club-house, of course, it is also an expensive hotel—if we may call it an hotel, and not rather a monastic settlement; for the inhabitants of these pleasant rooms all live for one end—golf: twice daily they go round the course, with all the leisurely solemnity of Benedictines reciting their office, and every night they meet in corona to discuss the mysteries of their religion.

Which reminds me that I have forgotten to mention the village Church. There is still a village, that straggles mysteriously, like so many English villages, in the form of a hollow square. In the old days, the Church interposed itself between the village and the Great House, a kind of mercy-seat through which the squire could be appeased upon occasion. Though much older than the Park or the fortunes of the Oatvile family, it had acquired, from its enclosed position, the air of a parasitical institution, an undergrowth of Protestant feudalism. Today, it somehow strikes the eye as a by-product of the golfing industry; people who ask the way to it (and they are rare) are directed to the fifteenth green; the service on Sunday is at half-past nine, so as to allow for the improbable chance of anybody wanting to fortify himself for the morning round by divine worship; the sexton will caddy for you except on the afternoon of a funeral. Conformably with this, the incumbent of the parish, who is to figure in this story, was a golfing parson presented by an absentee squire to a living which offered few material attractions. He had managed to let the parsonage, which was more than twenty minutes' walk from the first tee, and lived in the dormy-house permanently; arguing, not without reason, that it was the centre of all the life there was, in the parish. If you are disposed to take a look at him, you have only to open the smoking-room door; there he sits, this October afternoon of rain and fog, with three equally weatherbound companions, a foursome *in potentia*.

He was a man now approaching middle age, a bachelor and unambitious. You would say that he had a clerical face—is that clerical face a mark of predestination, or does it develop by natural mimicry?—but the enthusiasm which it registered was, it is to be feared, principally directed towards one object, and that object a game. He was mild-mannered, and had been known to keep his temper successfully in the most trying circumstances, even at the ninth; no oath was ever heard to escape his lips, though his invariable phrase, "What *tam* I doing?" was held by some to have a relish of perdition in it. The other three were acquaintances of his, as acquaintance goes at Paston Oatvile, where you know everybody's handicap, nobody's politics or religion. One of them, indeed, Alexander Gordon in nature and in name, could hardly be known otherwise than by his handicap, for in politics, in religion, in every subject that could form a digression from the normal conversation of the dormy-house, his point of view was entirely undistinguished and British to the last degree. He was not, like the others, a permanent inmate, but was on a holiday visit to his more interesting friend, Mordaunt Reeves.

Reeves was a permanent inmate, more by force of circumstances than from any natural indolence. He had left school at the beginning of the War, and had been incapacitated for active service by an extreme short-sightedness which gave his face a penetrating, not to say a peering, look. Work had been found for him easily enough in an outlying department of the War Office, and he was perhaps a little too fond of beginning his sentences with, "When I was in the Military Intelligence." The picture which the words conjured up to the uninitiated was that of Mordaunt Reeves concealed behind the arms with a revolver at half-cock, overhearing the confidential discussions of German super-spies. Actually, his business had been to stroll into a very uncomfortable office at half-past nine in the morning, where a docket of newspaper cuttings, forwarded from another department, awaited him. Singling out some particularly fire-eating utterance of a Glasgow shop-steward, he would have it typed out and put in a jacket; then he would scrawl across it: "Can something be done about this? Please initial"— and so the document would be caught up in that vast maelstrom of unregarded jackets that circulated aimlessly through the sub-departments of Whitehall. An orphan, with a comfortable income, he had found himself unable to settle down to ordinary employment on the outbreak of peace. He had put several romantic advertisements into the daily papers, indicating his readiness to undertake any mysterious commissions that might call for the services of an "active, intelligent young man, with a turn for the adventurous": but the supply of amateur adventurers was at the time well ahead of the demand, and there was no response. In despair, he had betaken himself to Paston Oatvile, and even his ill-wishers admitted that his game was improving.

That Mr. Carmichael, the fourth member of the

party, had been a don you knew as soon as he opened his mouth. There was that precision in his utterances, that benignity in his eye, that spontaneity in his willingness to impart information, that no other profession breeds. A perpetual fountain of interesting small-talk, he unnerved his audience with a sense of intellectual repletion which was worse than boredom. Not that he talked the "shop" of the learned: his subject had been Greek archaeology; his talk was of county families, of travels in the Near East, of the processes by which fountain-pens are manufactured, of county families again. He was over sixty—he, alone of the party was married, and lived in one of the bungalows with a colourless wife, who seemed to have been withered by long exposure to the sirocco of his conversation: at the moment she was absent, and he was lodging in the dormy-house like the rest. It must be confessed that his fellow-members shunned him, but he was useful upon occasion as a last court of appeal on any matter of fact; it was he who could remember what year it was the bull got loose on the links, and what ball the Open Championship was won with three years back.

Marryatt (that was the clergyman, yes; I see you are a proper reader for a detective-story) rose once more and took a good look at the weather. The fog was lifting, but the rain still fell pitilessly. "I shouldn't wonder," he said, "if we had some showers before nightfall."

"It's a curious thing," said Carmichael, "that

the early Basque poets always speak of the night not as falling but as rising. I suppose they had a right to look at it that way. Now, for myself——"

Marryatt, fortunately, knew him well enough to interrupt him. "It's the sort of afternoon," he said darkly, "on which one wants to murder somebody, just to relieve one's feelings."

"You would be wrong," said Reeves. "Think of the footmarks you'd be bound to leave behind you in mud like this. You would be caught in no time."

"Ah, you've been reading *The Mystery of the Green Thumb*. But tell me, how many murderers have really been discovered by their footprints? The bootmakers have conspired to make the human race believe that there are only about half a dozen different sizes of feet, and we all have to cram ourselves into horrible boots of one uniform pattern, imported by the gross from America. What does Holmes do next?"

"Well, you see," put in Gordon, "the detectives in the book always have the luck. The murderer generally has a wooden leg, and that doesn't take much tracing. The trouble in real life is the way murderers go about unamputated. And then there's the left-handed men, how conveniently they come in! I tried detection once on an old pipe, and I could show you from the way the side of it was charred that the owner of it was right-handed. But there are so many right-handed people."

"In most cases," said Carmichael, "it's only nerves that make people think they're left-handed. A more extraordinary thing is the matter of parting the hair. Everybody is predestined from birth to part his hair on one particular side; but most of the people who ought to part their hair on the right do it on the left instead, because that's easier when you're right-handed."

"I think you're wrong in principle, Gordon," said Reeves. "Everybody in the world has his little peculiarities, which would give him away to the eye of a trained detective. You, for example, are the most normal specimen, if I may say so, of the human race. Yet I know which of those whisky glasses on the mantelpiece is yours, though they're empty."

"Well, which?" asked Gordon, interested.

"The one in the middle," said Reeves. "It's pushed farther away from the edge: you, like the careful soul you are, instinctively took more precaution against its being brushed off. Aren't I right?"

"To tell the truth, I can't for the life of me remember. But there, you see, you're talking of somebody you know. None of us are murderers, at least, I hope not. If you were trying to detect a murderer you'd never been introduced to, you wouldn't know what to look out for."

"Try it on," suggested Marryatt. "You know, the Holmes stunt, deducing things from the bowler hat, and from Watson's brother's watch. Try that umbrella over there, whatever it's doing here; what will you deduce from it?"

"I should deduce that it had been raining recently," put in Gordon with great seriousness.

"As a matter of fact," said Reeves, turning the umbrella this way and that, "an umbrella's a very difficult thing to get any clues out of."

"I'm glad of that," said Carmichael, "because——"

"—only this one," continued Reeves, ignoring him, "happens to be rather interesting. Anybody could see that it's pretty new, yet the ferrule at the end of it is nearly worn through, which shows it's been used a lot. Inference: that it's used by somebody who doesn't keep his umbrella for days like this, but uses it as a walking-stick. Therefore it belongs to old Brotherhood; he's the only man I know in this club who always carries one."

"You see," said Carmichael, "that's the sort of thing that happens in real life. As I was just going to say, I brought in that umbrella myself. I took it by mistake from a complete stranger in the Tube."

Mordaunt Reeves laughed a little sourly. "Well," he said, "the principle holds, anyhow. Everything tells a story, if you are careful not to theorize beyond your data."

"I'm afraid," said Gordon, "I must be one of Nature's Watsons. I prefer to leave things where they lie, and let people tell me the story."

"There you are wrong," protested Reeves.

"People can never tell you a story without putting their own colour upon it—that is the difficulty of getting evidence in real life. There, I grant you, the detective stories are unreal: they always represent witnesses as giving the facts with complete accuracy, and in language of the author's own choosing. Somebody bursts into the room, and says, 'The body of a well-dressed man in middle-life has been found four yards away from the north end of the shrubbery. There are marks of violence about the person of the deceased'—just like a reporter's account of an inquest. But in real life he would say, 'Good God! A man's shot himself on the lawn'—leaping at once, you see, from observation to inference."

"Journalism," explained Carmichael, "makes havoc of all our detective stories. What is journalism? It is the effort to make all the facts of life correspond, whether they will or no, to about two hundred ready-made phrases. Head-lines are especially destructive—you will have noticed for yourselves how the modern head-line aspires to be a series of nouns, with no other parts of speech in attendance. I mean, the phrase, 'She went into the garden to cut a cabbage-leaf to make an apple pie' becomes 'Apple-pie fraud cabbage-leaf hunt,' and 'What; no soap! So he died' becomes 'Soap-shortage fatality sequel.' Under this treatment, all the nuances of atmosphere and of motive disappear; we figure the truth by trying to make it fit into a formula."

"I agree with you about inference," said Marryatt, disregarding Carmichael's last remark—one always did disregard Carmichael's last remark. "But think how much of one's knowledge of other people is really inference. What do we really know about one another down here? Fellow-passengers on the stream of life, that's all we are. Take old Brotherhood, whom you were mentioning just now. We know that he has some sort of business in London, but we've no idea what. We know that he comes down here every night in the week from Monday onwards, and then from Saturday to Monday he disappears—how do you know what he does with himself during the week-ends? Or take young Davenant down at the Hatcheries; he turns up there every Saturday evening, and does his two rounds on the Sunday, and then on Monday he's off again into the *Ewigkeit*. What do we really know about him?"

"I should have thought you knew all you wanted to about Brotherhood," chuckled Reeves. "Hasn't he taken to disproving the existence of God on Wednesday evenings on the village green?"

Marryatt flushed slightly. "After all," he said, "what does that amount to? You might as well say I know Davenant's a Roman Catholic. But all I know is that once in a way he goes over on a Sunday to Paston Bridge— the priest there knows something about him, I suppose, but he wouldn't tell you."

"I had a very extraordinary experience once,"

said Carmichael, "in Albania. I had to translate the confession of a dying man into French for the sake of a priest who didn't know the local language. The priest told me afterwards I was bound not to disclose to anybody what I'd heard."

"He didn't know you, anyhow, Carmichael," suggested Reeves.

"As a matter of fact, I've never mentioned what he said to anybody, though it was sufficiently curious."

"It's impossible," resumed Reeves, "not to make inferences; the mistake is to depend on them. In ordinary life, you have to take risks; you have to sit down in the barber's chair, although you know it is just as easy for him to cut your throat as to shave you. But in detection one should take no chances, give no one the benefit of the doubt. Half of the undetected crimes in the world are due to our reluctance to suspect anybody."

"But surely," urged Marryatt, "you would allow character to go for something? I was a schoolmaster once, and while one knew the little beasts were capable of almost anything, one did clear some people of suspicion, on mere character."

"But there again," argued Gordon, "you knew them very well."

"Not really," said Marryatt. "A perpetual war of mutual deception is kept up between schoolmasters and schoolboys. One trusted, I think, one's unconscious impressions most."

"If I were a detective," persisted Reeves, "I would suspect my own father or mother as soon as anybody else. I would follow up every clue, blinding myself deliberately to the thought, where does this point to?"

"Then you would be unreasonable," said Gordon. "In the old days, when the answers of sums used always to come out to an integral number—I believe it's all different now—one was wiser than that. If you could see that the answer was going to involve two-thirds of a policeman, you argued at once that you were on the wrong track; you started again, and suspected your working."

"But real life," retorted Reeves, "doesn't always work out to a simple answer. And if the policeman who's in charge of a case argues as you're arguing, he's only himself to blame for it if he gets trisected by the criminal before he's finished."

"At least you must respect the principle of *Cui bono?*"

"It's extraordinary," began Carmichael, "how many people make the old mistake about the meaning of—"

"*Cui bono* is the worst offender of the lot," said Mordaunt Reeves cheerfully. "Look at those two boys in America who murdered another boy just to find out what it felt like."

"But that was pathological."

"And how many crimes aren't pathological, if it comes to that?"

"I was on Holy Island once for a month," said Carmichael, "and would you believe it, there was a man there that was sick if he ever caught sight of a dog? Sick, positively."

"What do you think it really feels like," asked Marryatt, "to have murdered a man? I mean, murderers in general always seem to lose their heads when the thing is actually done, and give themselves away somehow. But one would have thought, if the thing is planned with proper deliberation, one's feeling would be that things were working out according to plan, and the next thing was to get clear—above all things, to see plenty of people, and to behave quite naturally in company."

"Why that?" asked Gordon.

"To establish your alibi. People are often careless about that."

"By the way," asked Carmichael, "did you bring a paper with you down from London? I'm interested to see the verdict in that Stanesby case. The young fellow is connected, I hear, with the Stanesbys of Martington."

"Afraid I left London at three, and that's too early for anything but betting tips. I say, you fellows, it's stopped raining."

CHAPTER II

IN THE ROUGH

THE view from the third tee was one which even a golfer might pause to admire. Let the Wordsworthian say what he will, railways ennoble our landscape; they give to our unassuming valleys a hint of motive and destination. More especially, a main line with four tracks pillowed on a sweep of tall embankment, that cannot cross a meandering country stream without a stilt-walk upon vast columns of enduring granite, captivates, if not the eye, at least the imagination. Such was the railway that stretched far into the distance, paralleling the course of your drive on the right: such was the great via-duct, some hundred feet ahead of you, that spanned laboriously, over four giant arches, the little river Gudgeon, most insignificant of streams. Shallow and narrow it ran, fringed by willow-herb and meadow-sweet, a paddling-place for cows and for unoccupied caddies. Here and there it threw out a patch of osiers—one in particular, that nestled at the foot of the railway-arches, was especially dreaded by golfers. In front, just visible above the railway where it receded northwards, were the thatched and tiled roofs of Paston Whitchurch, the next station down the line. To the right lay the old house, in its melancholy grandeur, behind it the village and church of Paston Oatvile. A superb avenue of elms connected the old house with the road between the two villages. The sun had newly come out, showing grass the greener and earth the browner for the late rain; elemental scents of turf and furrow greeted its restoration.

It may be doubted whether Mordaunt Reeves was particularly sensitive to such influences; if he was, it may have been this distraction which made him slice his drive. The ball dwindled down the gradual slope towards the river; cleared in a couple of bounds the tussocks of thick grass that dotted the little valley, and buried itself at last in the osier bed at the foot of the arches. Gordon and he—they were partners—set out at once to retrieve it, distrusting the efforts of an inefficient caddie, who was nearer the spot. It was only a closer view that showed how well-chosen a lair was this for a golf-ball hard pressed in the chase. The ground was all tussocks of rank grass, with hidden runlets that made islands of them; stubborn little shoots of willow arrested the searching club. They might have spent a full half-hour in vain scrutiny, had not Reeves's eye lighted suddenly on something he never looked to find there; a darker patch among the surrounding green, close to the foot of the first arch. It showed the outlines of a man.

A dog sleeps on the alert, with the visible threat of waking at any moment. A man's sleep is like the sleep of the horse; it imitates death. Reeves's first idea was that this man who lay so still must be a tramp who had strayed off the London highroad, and was taking his siesta in the lee of the viaduct. Then a gleam of more than military intelligence assured him that on such an afternoon of downpour a man composing himself to sleep would have been under the arch, not by the side of it. "Hello!" he shouted uneasily to Gordon, "looks as if there was something wrong here." Together they approached the prostrate body; it lay face downwards, and there was no movement of life. The thrill of distaste with which healthy nature shrinks from the sight of dissolution seized both of them. Gordon had served three years in the army, and had seen death; yet it was always death tricked out in the sacrificial garb of khaki; there was something different about death in a towncoat and striped grey trousers—it was a discord in the clear weather. The sun seemed to lose a shade of its brightness. Together they bent; and turned the body over, only to relinquish it again by a common instinct. Not only did the lolling head tell them that here the architecture of the human frame had been unknit; the face had disappeared, battered unrecognizably by some terrible and prolonged friction. They looked upwards, and knew at once that the sloping buttress of the arch, all of rough granite, must have intercepted a fatal fall, and added to its horror. Little about the head could be distinguished except closely-cut grey hair.

"Poor devil," said Gordon huskily. "Down from the line, I suppose."

"I say," said Reeves, "we mustn't let the caddie see this. Send him across to fetch the other two." Marryatt and Carmichael were now close behind them, and came up almost immediately.

"Is there somebody dead?" asked Marryatt. "I say, how awful." He kept on walking up and down as if thoroughly unnerved, repeating to himself, "How awful." Carmichael, for once, was dumb. It was a new voice that summed up the situation, in the words, " 'E's got 'is properly, ain't 'e?" and they turned round to find the caddie obviously enjoying a new sensation.

"Look here, we must move this somehow," suggested Gordon. "What about the tool-house under that arch?"

"I'm not quite sure I could lift it," said Reeves.

"That's all right, sir," said the caddie, "I'll whistle across to Ginger; in the scouts 'e was; they teach 'em what to do with bodies and that. 'Ere, Ginger!" and as his fellow-caddie approached, "Bloke fell off of the railway-line and smashed hisself up something cruel." Ginger whistled: "Dead, is 'e?" "Not half 'e ain't; shamming, that's what 'e is; go and 'ave a look at 'im."

Ginger satisfied his curiosity on the point; and these two cold-blooded young persons proceeded to hoist the body on to an ingenious arrangement of sticks, and so carried it off, under Gordon's directions, to the tool-house.

As the spell of the uncanny presence was removed, Reeves's horrified embarrassment ebbed from him a little, and left him with the sense that he ought to take command of the proceedings.

"Where's Beazly likely to be?" he asked—Beazly was the doctor.

"He went out in the rain," said Marryatt; "I should say he'd be about the tenth or eleventh by now. Look here, I'll nip across and get him," and in a moment he was running across the fairway.

"Seemed glad to get away," said Reeves; "well, it's too late for visiting the sick, and too soon for burying the dead. Carmichael, you're looking a bit on edge, too; would you mind going across to Paston Whitchurch, station and 'phoning up the police? Binver, I suppose, is the nearest place to get a bobby from. You will? Good." And as Carmichael too made off, "Look here, Gordon, what are we going to do about it? I've got the feeling that there's something wrong here. What do you say to doing a bit of detective work on our own—or are you feeling rotten?"

"Oh, I'm feeling all right," said Gordon, "only what about the police? Won't they want to look through the man's things first? It would be awkward if we put ourselves on the wrong side of the law. Funny thing, I've no idea whether there's any law against searching a dead body; yet, if there isn't, how do the police ever get their clues?"

"Oh, rot, the police can't be here for a good half-hour, and Beazly won't mind if he comes along. Let's take a bit of a look round, anyhow. He fell off the arch, and smashed up his face against the buttress, that looks pretty clear. Now, did he fall off the line, or off a train?"

"If you ask me, I should say he fell off the parapet. I've noticed, sometimes, what a long way it really is from the door of one's carriage to the parapet—a man falling from a carriage would never reach the edge."

"Ah," said Reeves, looking up, "but you're imagining the train stationary. He would be hurled forward some way by the impetus, if he jumped off a moving train. And I should say he could have started falling down that bank to the right, just before the parapet begins. He'd roll forwards and sideways, if you see what I mean, till he got to where the stonework begins, up there, and then, plop."

"I dare say you're right. Anyhow, we'd better be quick and look at the body."

As they went towards the tool-house, Reeves gave a sudden exclamation. "By Jove, his hat! And it's—let's see—I should say fifteen yards to the north of the body. Now why?"

"How do you mean?"

"There was no wind this afternoon. If his hat fell with him, it would lie with him. If it lies a dozen yards away, that looks as if—as if it was thrown after him. The considerate fellow-passenger hardly does that, does he?"

"You mean there's been dirty work?"

"I mean it looks as if there'd been dirty work. Now for the tool-shed."

To search a dead body is not an easy performance, unless you are in a hurry and have got to do it. Gordon did most of the work, and Reeves checked his results for him. The pockets contained a handkerchief, marked with the name "Masterman," a cigarette-case, of a common pattern, containing a cigarette of a brand smoked by every second man in the neighbourhood, a half-empty box of matches, a pipe and an empty pouch, two florins, a letter and a business communication both addressed to S. Brotherhood, Esq., and a watch and chain. They also found, written on the back of the letter, a pencilled list of goods, as if to remind a man of his shopping needs.

"It's a queer thing," said Reeves, "that watch; because he's got one on his wrist too. How many people, I wonder, carry a stomach-watch as well as a wrist-watch? It's stopped, I suppose?"

"Blessed if it isn't going! An hour fast, apparently, but going. Good advertisement for the makers, what?"

"But the wrist-watch?"

"That's stopped."

"When?"

"Six minutes to five."

"What did I say about trains? The 4.50 from Paston Oatvile would be just passing here at six minutes to five. How's that for deduction?"

"Looks all right, anyhow. And, by Gad, here's a third single from town to Paston Whitchurch. Is to-day the sixteenth? Yes, then that's quite on the square. Now, stand by while I see if his clothes are marked."

But neither coat nor shirt, neither collar nor trousers bore any mark of ownership. The suit was from Messrs. Watkins in New Oxford Street, the shirt and collar were of a brand which it would be mere advertisement to mention. During all this time, Reeves was making a transcript of the three documents, not without a certain sense of intrusion upon a dead man's confidence. As Gordon began to look into one of the boots, Reeves gave a whisper of warning, and a policeman (for they have motorcycles even in the police force) came into distant view. Panic seized the forces of Baker Street, and (forgetting that they had a perfect right to be in charge of the dead man's body) they resumed, very shamefacedly, their search for the lost ball. It seemed incongruous somehow, to be worrying about a golf-ball— ought there to be a local rule about what happened if you found a corpse on the links? Certainly the game had been abandoned, and the caddies, to their great regret, sent back with the clubs.

"Good evening, gentlemen," said the policeman, eyeing them narrowly. It was not that he suspected them or anybody of anything; he merely sized them up by force of habit to see whether they were the kind of people you touched your hat to or the kind of people you told to move on. The scrutiny being favourable, he allowed them to slash about in the undergrowth and watch, with ill-concealed curiosity, the official proceedings of Scotland Yard.

Scotland Yard did very much what they had done, only with a splendidly irrelevant thoroughness. Not only the destination, class, and date of the ticket had to be registered in the notebook, but its price—there even seemed to be a moment's hesitation about the Company's regulations on the back. Nor did the names of the cigarette-importer and the collar-maker go unrecorded; both watchmakers, the post-marks on the correspondence, the date on the florins—nothing escaped this man. Tired of waiting for the doctor and the inevitable ambulance, Gordon and Reeves abandoned the truant ball, and made their way thoughtfully to the dormy-house.

Wilson, the club gossip, met them at the entrance. "Heard about old Brotherhood?" he asked, and went on, before they had time to gasp: "He's gone bankrupt; heard it to-day in the City."

"Really?" said Reeves. "Come and have a drink." But if he thought that he too had the telling of a story, he was mistaken; the door opened on a well-known voice:

"Yes, sliced his drive badly, did Reeves. A curious thing, that,—you 'slice' a ball in golf and you 'cut' a ball at cricket, and it's the same action in either case, and yet it's nothing whatever to do with the motion of cutting a cake. What was I saying? Oh yes. Right against the viaduct—did you ever see the big viaduct they've got at Welwyn? A finer one than ours, even—he found . . ."

Which made it evident that Mr. Carmichael was telling, in his own way, the story of the day's adventure.

CHAPTER III

PIECING IT TOGETHER

IF the general accommodation at the Paston Oatvile dormy-house cannot be described as cloistral, it must be admitted that the rooms in it where you can claim privacy are not much better than cells. Mordaunt Reeves, however, had done something to turn his apartments into a civilized dwelling-place; there were pictures which did not illustrate wings, and books devoted to other subjects than the multitudinous possibilities of error in playing golf. Gordon and he had each a comfortable arm-chair, each a corner of the fire-place to flick his cigarette-ash into, when they met that evening to talk over the possibilities of the situation as it had hitherto developed.

"Everybody," said Reeves, "if you notice, has already started treating an assumption as if it were a fact. They all say it was Brotherhood we found lying there; they all say he committed suicide because he had just gone bankrupt. Now, as a matter of fact, we don't know that it was Brotherhood at all. He has not been heard of, but there hasn't been much time to hear of him; and nothing is more probable than that a man who has gone bankrupt should skip without leaving any traces."

"Yes, but somebody's dead; you've got to find a gap somewhere in the ranks of Society to match our corpus."

"Still, that's mere negative arguing. And there are several points that tell against its being Brotherhood. In the first place, that ticket. Brotherhood goes up and down every day; do you mean to tell me he hasn't got a season? Second point, if it was Brotherhood there's an odd coincidence—he died within ten minutes' walk of his own bungalow; why there, any more than anywhere else on the line?"

"It's a coincidence that Brotherhood should be killed so near his own bungalow. But the murder, whether we like it or not, has been committed just there, so I don't see why it shouldn't be him as much as anybody else. However, go on."

"Third point, the handkerchief. Why should Brotherhood be carrying somebody else's handkerchief?"

"If it comes to that, why should somebody else be carrying Brotherhood's correspondence?"

"Oh, Brotherhood is mixed up in it somehow right enough. We shall see. Next point to be considered, was it accident, suicide, or murder?"

"You can cut out accident, surely. That *would* be a coincidence—somebody carrying Brotherhood's letter to fall out of the train by mere accident just where Brotherhood lives."

"Very well, for the present we'll ask Murder or Suicide? Now, I've several arguments against suicide.

First, as I told you, the hat. He wasn't alone when he fell out of the carriage, or who threw the hat after him?"

"There was no mark in the hat, was there?"

"Only the maker's; that's the irritating thing about this business. Hats, collars, shirts, people buy them at a moment's notice and pay cash for them, so there's no record in the books. And watches—of course you don't have a watch sent, you take it with you, to save the danger of carriage by post. I'll try all those tradesmen if the worst comes to the worst; probably the police have already; but I bet nothing comes of it."

"What's your next argument against suicide?"

"The ticket. That extra four bob would have got him a first instead of a third. Now, a man who means to commit suicide doesn't want four bob, but he does want to be alone."

"But the suicide might have been an impulse at the last moment."

"I don't believe it. The place where he fell was just the one place about here where he was bound to kill himself, not merely maim himself. That looks like preparation."

"All right. Any more?"

"No, but I think that's enough to go on with. The probability I'm going to bet on is murder."

"You're up against coincidence again, though, there. Why should somebody happen to murder Brotherhood on the very day he went bankrupt?"

"You *will* go on assuming that it is Brotherhood. Supposing, just for the sake of argument, that Brotherhood has saved a nest-egg for himself, and is skipping to avoid his creditors—what better way of throwing people off the scent than by a pretended suicide?"

"That is, by pitching a total stranger down the viaduct."

"I didn't say a total stranger. Suppose it were somebody in pursuit of him, or somebody he suspected of pursuing him?"

"But he couldn't be sure that the face would get mangled like that. It was only one chance in a thousand that the body should scrape down all along that buttress on its face."

"He may simply have wanted to kill the man, without hoping that the corpse would be mistaken for him. After all, we've got to explain the ticket; a man who takes a single ticket down here is almost certainly not a resident here—the half-fare is so cheap. A spy, tracking him, or somebody he takes to be a spy tracking him. He stuns the man while he's not looking, and then pitches him out. He's desperate, remember."

"Well, it seems to hang together that way."

"But I'm not at all sure that's the right way. I'm not at all sure that Brotherhood isn't the murderee, and the murderer somebody unknown—such a murder might be connected with a bankruptcy, a ruined creditor, for example."

"And how are you going to look for the murderer if that's so?"

"You're going to help me. We're going to have a little detective holiday, and leave the game alone for a bit. Of course we must find out all about Brotherhood first—it's extraordinary how little people seem to know about him. I asked four men in the Club whether he wore a wrist-watch or not: two couldn't remember, one said he did, and one swore he didn't. But there must be some servant who looks after his bungalow for him; so I'm going there to-morrow to pump them."

"Introducing yourself as Mr. S. Holmes of Baker Street, or how?"

"No, I shall be the *Daily Mail* reporter—unless I run into the real article on the mat. Now, would you mind following up the Masterman clue?"

"What Masterman clue?"

"There are only two Mastermans in the Telephone Directory. A man dressed like that would be sure to have a telephone."

"But I thought you'd made up your mind it wasn't a local person at all, because of the ticket?"

"I know, it's probably a wild-goose chase, but it's the best we can do on that tack. Both are at Binver; one's a solicitor and one a doctor. I'll give you the addresses."

"And I'm to go to them and ask them what kind of handkerchiefs they use? Or should I meet them accidentally and say, Excuse me, sir, could you lend me a handkerchief, I've left mine at home?"

"Well, you can find out whether they're dead, anyhow."

"And if they're still alive?"

"Well, scout around somehow. Do anything that occurs to you. This business ought to be rather fun, if we exercise a little ingenuity."

"Meanwhile, let's have another look at those documents. We don't seem to have made much out of them, and that's a fact."

They sat for several minutes in silence, re-reading the copy Reeves had made of the anonymous letter. It was undated; the address was in printed capitals; it had been post-marked in London at starting, and at Paston Whitchurch on arrival. The content of the message was a mere series of numbers, as follows:

8	7	5
18	4	7
21	2	3
25	6	4
31	4	8
74	13	9
92	29	7
97	5	3
113	17	13
10	12	13

"Unless they're sums of money," said Gordon, "I can't make head or tail of it all. And if they were sums of money, it would be a queer way to arrange the spacing."

"Wait one moment," said Reeves, "I believe I've got the idea of it." He put his hand to his forehead. "Yes, that does it. It's a cipher, of course, otherwise there'd be something to explain what it's all about. It will be a book cipher; the first figure gives you the page, the second the line, and the third the word in the line. How's that?"

"That's devilish ingenious," admitted Gordon, "but you can hardly prove it."

"I can practically prove it," said Reeves. "Look here, the man wanted to spell out a message in ten words. There was a book, arranged upon somehow beforehand. The first few words were ordinary words, that you could find anywhere on any page: and naturally, to save himself and the other man trouble in counting, he took them from the top of the page, so you get lines 7, 4, 2, 6, and 4 of pages 8, 18, 21, 25 and 31. The sixth word he wanted was an obscure sort of word, perhaps even a proper name. He had to go right on to page 74, and even then he could only find his word on the 13th line of it. Then the next two words came easy, comparatively, but the ninth word was a brute, he couldn't find it till page 113, and on the 17th line at that. And by that time he'd got nearly to the end of the book—a book, then, of only 120 pages or so probably; a paper edition, I suspect—so he had to go back to the beginning again, which he hadn't meant to do."

"Bravo!" said Gordon. "Have another injection of cocaine."

"The curse of the thing is," said Mordaunt Reeves, "that with a book cipher you can't possibly guess the message unless you've got the book. I think we shall have to establish the identity before we get any further on that tack. Let's have a look at the letter now."

The letter was a curt official communication from the Railway Company, only the details being filled in in ink, the rest a mere printed form:

London Midland and Scottish Railway.

10. 10. 19XY.

Dear Sir,

I beg to acknowledge receipt of your letter of 9th instant and have given orders for a berth to be reserved in the sleeping car attached to the 7.30 train on Thursday (corrected to Wednesday) the 18th (corrected to 17th) of October to Glasgow. I note that you will join the train at Crewe.
S. Brotherhood Esq.

"These corrections are rummy," said Reeves. "I wonder if perhaps Brotherhood's letter corrected itself in a postscript? You see, assuming that Brotherhood was skipping, it's all right for him to go to Glasgow—rather ingenious, in fact—but why shouldn't he travel to-night, the sixteenth, instead of to-morrow night?"

"He couldn't get away early enough. Or could he? Got a Bradshaw?" Gordon proceeded to look up the trains with an irritating thoroughness, while Reeves danced with impatience—there is no impatience like that engendered by watching another man look up Bradshaw. "That's all right," said Gordon at last. "In order to catch the Scottish train at Crewe he'd have had to take that earlier train, the one Marryatt came up by, and get out at Binver. He took the 3.47, I suppose, because he couldn't get away sooner. Perhaps, if we're right in thinking he wanted to skip, he was going to go across country by car to-morrow and confuse his tracks a bit."

"The thing doesn't look like skipping quite as much as it did. For Heaven's sake let's beware of prejudicing the case. Anyhow, he meant to make for Glasgow on the Wednesday night—that's tomorrow night, isn't it? Now let's have one more look at that silly list that was on the back of the anonymous letter."

The list had been copied almost in facsimile, for it was very short. It ran

> Socks
> vest
> hem
> tins—

at least, that was the general impression it gave, but the writing was so spidery as to make it very doubtful which precise letter each of the strokes represented.

"I suppose it must be a shopping-list of some sort. If one could make that last word 'ties' it would read better," said Gordon.

"But even so you wouldn't have hems in a shopping-list."

"It might be ham."

"But one doesn't buy ham at the hosier's."

"And why did he write at the edge of the paper like that?"

"If it comes to that, who was the he? It's not Brotherhood's writing—I've verified that from the club book. I fancy this goes pretty deep. Look here, here's a bit of detection for you. That sheet has been torn off at the left-hand side, hasn't it? Now, was it torn off before or after the writing was put on it?"

"Before, surely. Otherwise the initial letters wouldn't be so complete; he'd have been certain to tear across them."

"I'm not so sure. Who writes so close to the edge of a piece of paper as that? Remember, I copied the thing down exactly, and each word was close up against the tear."

"I don't quite see what difference it makes, anyhow," objected Gordon.

"More than you think, perhaps. I shouldn't wonder if this bit of paper turned up trumps, when we've thought it over a bit more. But there's one thing that fairly beats me."

"What's that?"

"Those two watches. It doesn't seem to me to make any sense. Well, we'd better get to bed and sleep over it."

CHAPTER IV

ENDLESS CLUES

THERE is no surer soporific than sleeping over a problem, no more fallacious method of attempting a solution. After murmuring to himself three times, "Let's see; there was something about watches," Mordaunt Reeves fell into a sleep which anybody but a psychoanalyst would have called dreamless. He woke in the morning with a strong resolution to do the ninth in four, which melted through lazy stages of half-awareness into the feeling that there was something else to do first. The adventures of yesterday, the duties of to-day, returned to him. He was already nearly dressed when he remembered that he had decided on the rôle of a *Daily Mail* reporter for his morning's investigation, and grimly set himself to remove again the bulging knickerbockers and the hypocritical garters of his kind. Dressy they might be, but they were not Fleet Street. His memories of the reporter's wardrobe were, it must be confessed, somewhat disordered, and he was greeted in the breakfast-room with flippant inquiries whether he had gone into mourning for the Unknown Passenger.

He found Gordon already at table with Marryatt—Marryatt in the high clerical collar which was irreverently known to his intimates as "New every morning."

"Well, how are you feeling?" he asked. "You looked rather chippy yesterday. However, I suppose it brings a job of work your way."

"Confound it," said Marryatt, "that's the trouble. The jury at the inquest are bound to bring in suicide; and then I can't bury the man in the churchyard, and all the villagers will say I refused out of spite, because the poor old chap used to give these atheist lectures on the village green."

"Rot!" said Gordon; "if they do find suicide, they'll certainly say he was of unsound mind."

"Yes," echoed Reeves, "if they do bring in suicide."

"But surely you can't doubt it," urged Marryatt energetically. "The man's just gone bankrupt, and it was an ugly case, from what I hear; several innocent people who'd been fools enough to believe in him left in the cart. At the same time, the smash came very suddenly, and that makes it unlikely that anybody could want to murder the man so soon. Oh, you'll find it's suicide right enough."

"Well," said Reeves a little stiffly, "we're going to do our best to find out between us. I've the greatest respect for the police as a body, but I don't think they're very good at following up clues. When I was in the Military Intelligence one was constantly putting material at the disposal of the police which they were too supine or too stupid to use."

"Well, good luck to your sleuthing; but mark my

words, you'll find it was suicide. I'm going to play a round now to try and take my mind off the thing, but I don't believe I shall be able to drive at the third after— after what we saw yesterday."

Left to themselves, Mordaunt Reeves and Gordon arranged that they would meet again at luncheon and report on the morning's investigations.

"And look here," said Reeves, "it's a belief of mine that one wants to cover the ground oneself if one's to visualize the setting of a crime properly. So I vote that after lunch we stroll down to the railway and take a look at the top of that viaduct, and then take the 4.50 from Paston Oatvile to Paston Whitchurch so as to picture the whole thing exactly as it happened." And so they parted, Reeves walking to Brotherhood's bungalow, close to Paston Whitchurch station, while Gordon mounted a motor-bicycle and set out for Binver, a sleepy market town of some importance as a railway junction, about twelve miles off.

Mr. Brotherhood's housekeeper, Mrs. Bramston, had something of the airs of a landlady. She spoke painfully correct English, far more terrible than the native cockney which it half revealed and half concealed. She commenced where others began, closed doors where others shut them, and recollected instead of remembering. Her final consonants were all sibilant, and seemed to form part of the succeeding word. She was a merciless and largely irrelevant talker, and the opportunity of a stranger's visit delighted her, self-importance easily triumphing over any regret she may have felt for the apparently deceased. She had no doubt that Reeves was a reporter, but it is probable that she would have opened out quite as readily if he had announced himself as the piano-tuner.

"From the *Daily Mail?* To be sure, sir. I'm always fond of looking at a paper myself, and as for the *Daily Telegraph*, I simply revel in it. Called about poor Mr. Brotherood, I suppose; well, there isn't much doubt what's come to him, poor soul . . . Not Mr. Brotherood at all? Don't you delude yourself, young man; that's him, sure enough. The police, they wanted me to go and look at the corpse; but I didn't hardly like to; battered they say it was, something shocking. His clothes? Of course they were his clothes; you don't think he'd want to be putting somebody else's clothes on to commit suicide in, do you? That's the same as he always wore; plain black coat and grey striped trousers, just the same as it was in the papers. . . . What tailor he went to? No, I couldn't rightly say that; though I've had the folding of them many a time; very neat man he was, Mr. Brotherhood, in his personal habits. Oh, I dare say there's others as have clothes like his, only you see the way I look at it is, if the clothes were *on* Mr. Brotherood, then it's Mr. Brotherood's clothes they'll be, that's the way I look at it.

"A single gentleman? Yes, a single gentleman he was,

single and singular, if you'll pardon the *jeu de mots*. Very singular in his habits. Every Saturday off he'd go, just the same as it was in the papers, and where he went to is more than I can say, though I've been looking after him the best part of a year now. Every afternoon from Monday to Saturday he'd come home by the five o'clock train, and then he'd go for his round of golf, and I'd have a bit of cold supper ready for him when he came home . . . .

"No, I can't say that I've noticed anything strange about him of late. You see, he was always a very reserved gentleman, Mr. Brotherood was very silent, if you understand what I mean, in conversation." (Reeves felt that this was probably a characteristic common to most of Mrs. Bramston's interlocutors.) "Time and again he's said to me would I mind leaving him now because he'd got a great deal to do. I recollect about a fortnight ago he did seem rather put out about not being able to find his overcoat when he went out to deliver his address to the villagers; but I found it for him . . . . No, it isn't much more than two months ago since he commenced exhorting. I never could see what he did it for; not that I go to church myself, but you see the way I look at it is if people want to go to church why not let them go to church? Live and let live, that's what I say. I shouldn't call myself a religious woman, mind you, but I like to see everyone go their own way, and not leave tracts. Miss Frobisher she used to come here with tracts, but I said to her, 'Miss Frobisher,' I said, 'you're wasting your time leaving tracts here,' and so she was. . . .

"Mad, sir? Oh dear no, not what you could call mad. Of course we all have our own little ways, haven't we, sir? and as I was telling you, Mr. Brotherood was singular, but not demented; I should never have stopped with Mr. Brotherhood had he been demented . . . . Suicide? Of course it was suicide; and there's some say Mr. Marryatt won't bury him in holy ground, don't they? Well, you take my word for it, Mr. Brotherood wouldn't mind about a little thing like that. Some people seem not to mind *what* happens to them once they're gone: Mr. Bramston was like that, while he was spared to me; never seemed to mind if we were to take a spade and bury him in the back garden, that's the way *he* looked at it. But of course, I wouldn't have that, and he was buried properly in holy ground, Mr. Bramston was, and the minister recited the service over him beautiful. . . . What, must you be going already, sir? Well, I'm sure it's been a great privilege to me to afford you information. Good morning, sir."

This is an abridged account of the interview, but it contains all the material disclosures made by Mrs. Bramston. Reeves found himself pitying the coroner who would have to face and to stem that seething torrent of conversation. He came back to the dormy-house to find that it was already nearly time for luncheon, and Gordon was waiting for him, returned from his errand at Binver.

"Well, have you found out anything?" asked Gordon.

"Yes," said Reeves, "I've found a wife for Carmichael. I've found a woman who could give him a stroke a hole at back-chat." And he launched into a description of Mrs. Bramston's voluminous utterance and her insignificant contribution to the solving of the mystery.

"Had you any better luck?" he went on.

"Acting upon instructions received, I proceeded first of all to the offices of Messrs. Masterman, Formby and Jarrold, Solicitors. It's one of those jolly old Queen Anne houses facing on the High Street; with a flagged walk up to the front door and blue gates that need painting— or rather, it would spoil them if you did. It's been turned into an office, and the inside is all musty and smells of decaying paper. The mustiest thing there was the old clerk I went up to and asked if I could see Mr. Masterman. And he said, 'I'm afraid not, sir; Mr. Masterman is dead.' "

"Dead? How? When?"

"My very words. And the old gentleman said, 'About twenty-three years ago. Would you like to see Mr. Jarrold?' Well, that did me in rather, because even if old Masterman did bequeath his handkerchiefs to Jarrold, it isn't likely that old Jarrold would be still using them, though they would about match his furniture if he did."

"How did you get out of it? You were rather badly placed."

"I was, and I cursed you pretty freely. However, I extricated myself without any heart-to-heart talks with Mr. Jarrold. I just said, 'I'm so sorry, I must have made some mistake; this is *Doctor* Masterman's house, isn't it?' That killed two birds with one stone, I eluded suspicion and also got directed to the other Masterman house, a big house, the man said, at the other end of the water-meadow behind the church."

"So you went on there?"

"No; it occurred to me that a man who lived in a house that size probably kept a man-servant or two, and it was up to me to personate one of them. So I went round to the Binver Steam Laundry, where I'm not known personally; and said I was from Dr. Masterman's, and could they be kind enough to inform Dr. Masterman as to what action they intended taking about the twelve last handkerchiefs that hadn't come back from the wash. That sounds risky, but it wasn't really, because all men think they've more clothes at the wash than they really have. The lady in charge was quite patient and kind, obviously well accustomed to that sort of complaint; she said all Dr. Masterman's handkerchiefs had been sent back. Fortunately I bluffed, and insisted upon a search; after a bit she came and put into my hands a pile of handkerchiefs, which I took away with me. There were five of them, four Mastermans and a Brotherhood."

"Oh! That rather looks as if——"

"Exactly; it looks as if we ought to have recognized the touch of the Binver Steam Laundry. In fact, it would be very suspicious in these parts if you found a dead man wearing one of his own handkerchiefs. Well, there seemed no point in keeping any of them, so I dropped the lot into Masterman's letter-box. Unusual, perhaps, but I felt it would save explanations."

"Well, I'm sure we're all very grateful to Mr. Gordon for his splendid work among the Mastermen. But it begins to look as if we were left very much where we were. We still don't even know who the corpse was."

There was a knock at the door, and the unwelcome figure of Carmichael obtruded itself. "Sorry if I interrupt," he said, "but I thought you might be interested in this poor fellow we found yesterday. My caddie this morning was giving me the latest news. It's extraordinary how these-caddies pick up everything except one's ball."

"What news?" gasped Reeves.

"Well, it seems that Brotherhood was insured at one of these American offices. And they're a great deal more particular than our own Insurance people. And after all they're right to be: one's so apt to think of the Insurance Company as a set of sharks, when in reality they are only protecting the interests of their policy-holders."

"Granted," said Gordon. "Proceed."

"Well, as soon as they heard of the bankruptcy and then saw the news in the morning paper about the Links Tragedy, the Insurance Company pricked up its ears. Apparently, in the actuarial world, bankruptcy followed by alleged suicide is a matter of daily occurrence, and they have their suspicions. That is why I say they are quite within their rights when they insist upon registering a man by his birth-marks before they insure him. It's an extraordinary thing about birth-marks; we really know nothing about them——"

"Nor want to," said Reeves, "for the time being. What happened?"

"I was just telling you. A man came down from the Insurance Company to identify the corpse; and my caddie heard about it from——"

"Heard what?"

"Why, that it *is* Brotherhood. They recognized him from the birth-mark."

"So that's that," said Mordaunt Reeves, a little bitterly. "Trust the Insurance people not to make a mistake. I confess that, after the handkerchief clue failed, I had begun to think it must be Brotherhood who was dead. I suppose your caddie didn't happen to mention whether it was suicide or murder?"

"He assumed it to be suicide; but not, I think, with any inside information. Of course, it was a foggy day. Did you know that, as a matter of statistics, there are more suicides in November than in any other month?"

"I will make a note of the fact," said Mordaunt Reeves.

CHAPTER V

ON THE RAILWAY

THE afternoon seemed a compensation for yesterday; October sun glowed temperately over the links, with the air of a kind old gentleman producing sweetmeats unexpectedly. The rich but transient gold of summer evenings seemed hoarded in this summer of St. Luke; the air not over-charged with uneasy heat, but lucid and caressing; the leaves no longer in the shock of their summer finery, but dignified in the decayed gentility of their autumn gold. A perfect day for golf, such was the immediate impression of the Paston Oatvile mind; but to Reeves a second thought occurred— it was a bad day for following up the clues of a murder.

"It's all very well," he said to Gordon, "the visibility's good, and we shan't be interrupted by rain; but we can't get the atmosphere; the spiritual atmosphere, I mean, of yesterday's fog and drizzle. We shall see where a man fell down the embankment, but we shan't feel the impulse of that weeping depression which made him throw himself over, or made somebody else save him the trouble. We haven't got the *mise-en-scène* of a tragedy."

They climbed together, Gordon and he; a zigzag

path up the side of the huge embankment, close to the club-house. When it reached the level of the line, it kept close to the trim hedge that marked the boundary of the railway's property, and so lasted till the very beginning of the viaduct, where it dives under the first arch at a precarious angle and came up the other side. It was a matter of common knowledge to the good-humoured porters of Paston Oatvile that the shortest way from that station to the neighbouring station of Paston Whitchurch was along the railway line itself—the shortest, because it avoided the steep dip into the valley. Accordingly, it was the habit of residents, if pressed for time, to follow this path up to the viaduct, then to break over the sacred hedge and walk over the railway bridge till a similar path was available on the Paston Whitchurch side. This local habit Reeves and Gordon now naturally followed, for it gave them access to the very spot from which, twenty-four hours before, a human body had been hurled down on to the granite buttress and the osier-bed that lay beneath.

"You see what I mean," said Reeves. "We can't, of course, tell what pace the train was going; they vary so much in the fog. But if, for the sake of argument, you take the force with which I throw this stone as the impetus of the train, you see how the curve of the slope edges it out to the right—there—and it falls either exactly on the buttress or next door to it. That's how I picture yesterday afternoon—the man takes a good jump—or gets a

good shove, and falls just over the edge; there's nothing
for him to catch on to; and between his own motion and
the slope of the embankment he gets pitched on to the
buttress. I don't know any place along this line where
the drop comes so close. The coroner will call attention
to that—it's extraordinary the way coroners do draw
attention to all the least important aspects of the case. I
read a newspaper account once of a man who was killed
by a motor-car just as he came out of church, and I'm
blessed if the coroner didn't draw attention to the
dangerous habit of standing about outside churches."

"I must say, the place seems made for something like
this happening. Do you see how the line curves away
from this side?"

"Why shouldn't it?"

"What I mean is, it would be very hard for anybody
to see Brotherhood fall out of the train unless he was
travelling in the same coach: the other coaches would
be out of view (unless a man were leaning right out of
the window), simply owing to the curve—and of course
a fog would make the job all the easier."

"By Jove, that's true. I must say, I stick to my murder
theory, whatever the jury make of it. In fact, I hope they
will bring in suicide, because then the police won't be
fussing round all over the place. It looks to me like a
murder, and a carefully planned one."

"I'd just like to try your stone-throwing trick

once more. Look here, I'll lean over the edge and watch it fall. Only we shall want a bigger stone, if you can find one."

"All right. Only they're all little ones between the sleepers. I'll look along the bank a bit. I say, what the devil's this?"

It was a sight that on most days would have given little surprise to the pair; a common enough sight, indeed, down in the valley, but up here a portent. Caught in a clump of grass, some twenty yards down the line in the Paston Oatvile direction, was a golf-ball.

"That beats everything," declared Gordon. "I don't believe Carmichael on his worst day could slice a ball a hundred feet up in the air and lodge it in that clump."

Reeves was examining the trove intently. "I don't like this a bit," he said. "This is practically a new ball, not the sort of ball a man would throw away casually as he walked down the line. A Buffalo, I see—dash it all, there are at least a dozen of us use those. Who'll tell us whether Brotherhood used them?"

"I say, steady on! You've got this murder business on the brain. How can you tell the ball hasn't been there weeks and weeks?"

"Very simply, because it happens to have snapped the stalk of this flower—scabious, don't they call 'em—which isn't dead yet. The ball was right on top when I found it. I'm hanged if that ball fell there more than twenty-four hours ago."

"I say, we ought to be getting back to Oatvile if we're going to catch that train," said Gordon. "It's half-past four already, and we've got to take to the path before we come in sight of the signal-box. The signalman doesn't really mind, but he has to pretend to."

Gordon was one of those men who are always too early for trains. As a matter of fact they got into Paston Oatvile station before the 3.47 from London was signalled. The 4.50 from Paston Oatvile had to connect with it for the sake of passengers going on to Paston Whitchurch or Binver, and was still wandering up and down in a siding, flirting with a couple of milk-vans and apparently enjoying itself. The platform was nearly bare of passengers, a fact on which Reeves artfully commented to an apathetic porter.

"Not many travelling? You wait till the London train comes in, sir; there's always plenty in that as change here."

"I suppose it's the first train people can get away from business by, eh?"

"That's right, sir; there ain't nothing else stops here after the midday train. Of course there's the fast train to Binver, but that passes through 'ere. You travellin', sir?"

"Just to Binver. Hullo, there's the booking-office opening at last. D'you mind getting two firsts for Binver, Gordon? Very sad thing that, about Mr. Brotherhood," he went on to the porter.

"That's right, sir; very melancholy thing, sir."

"I suppose you didn't see him get on to the train?"

"There's such a lot of 'em, sir, you don't notice 'em, not the ones that travel every day. And Mr. Brotherhood, 'e was a man as 'adn't many words for anybody. Though of course there's some as is different; d'you know Mr. Davenant, sir, up at the Hatcheries? He's a nice gentleman, that is, has a word for everybody. I seed 'im getting off of the London train, and 'e asked me after my bit of garden—nothing stuck-up about 'im. Excuse me, sir." And, as the London train swung into view, he proceeded up and down the platform making a noise something like Paston Oatvile, for the information of anybody who could not read notice-boards.

The London train was undeniably full to overflowing, and even when the Paston Oatvile residents had diminished the number, there were enough waiting for the Paston Whitchurch and Binver train to leave no compartment unoccupied. Even in their first-class carriage, it was only by luck that Reeves and Gordon managed to travel by themselves.

"I say," began Gordon, "why Binver? We don't want to go beyond Whitchurch, do we?"

"Oh, it's just an idea of mine. We can get a train back in time for dinner. Don't you come unless you'd like to. Steady, here we are." And they swept slowly past the scene they had just been viewing from the solid ground. Reeves opened the door a little as they passed, and threw out a fresh stone; he had the satisfaction of seeing it disappear exactly according to schedule. "Now," he said, "we've got a quiet quarter of an hour to spend before we get to Binver. And I'd be dashed glad if you'd tell me two things. First, how can anyone have planned and executed a murder in a third-class carriage on a train so infernally crowded as this one is?"

"They may have been travelling first. No one examines the tickets."

"But even so, look at the risks. We should have had that fat old party in here if I hadn't puffed smoke in her face, and there are very few firsts on the train. Our man took big chances, that's certain."

"And the other point?"

"Why did Davenant come up by this train yesterday? Of course you don't know the place as I do, but Davenant's a scratch player, and a bit of a local celebrity. Every child in the place knows that Davenant only comes down here for week-ends, and it's impossible to get a game with him except on Sunday. Why does he suddenly turn up on a Tuesday afternoon?"

"Well, I suppose he's a right to, hasn't he? I thought you were saying he has a cottage here?"

"Yes, but one's bound to notice every deviation from the normal when one's trying to trace causes. Look here, here's Whitchurch. Do you mind getting out and calling at the Hatcheries—that house, there—and finding out, on some excuse, when Davenant got there, and whether he's there now? You're not known, you see—but be devilish tactful; we don't want to put anybody on his guard."

"Right-o! more lying necessary, I foresee. Oh, what a tangled web we weave when first we practise to deceive. So long, Sherlock, meet you at dinner."

Reeves' errand, it appeared when he got to Binver, was once more with the railway staff. He went up to a porter, and said, "Excuse me, does this train get cleared out here? I mean, if one leaves a thing in the carriage, would it be taken out here?"

"That's right, sir. Left Luggage Office is what you want."

"Well, this was only a paper book. I thought perhaps you people cleared them away for yourselves, like the newspapers."

"Ah, if it was a paper book, we 'aven't any orders to take that on to the Left Luggage Office. We takes those away, mostly; what might the name of your book be, sir?"

This was not at all the question Reeves wanted, but he was prepared for it. "It was *The Sorrows of Satan*, by Miss Corelli," he said. "I left it in one of these carriages yesterday."

"Well, sir, I cleaned out this train yesterday myself, and there wasn't no book of that name. A passenger must have taken it out with them most likely. There wasn't not but one book I found in those carriages, and you're welcome to that, sir; I've got it on the seat there." And he produced a repellent-looking volume entitled *Formation of Character*, by J. B. S. Watson.

Reeves was trembling with excitement, but it was clearly not a case for showing any enthusiasm. "Well, give you sixpence for it," he said, and the porter willingly agreed—he had guessed rightly that the sixpence would prove to be half-a-crown.

It was an agony dawdling back by a slow train to Paston Oatvile, knowing that he could not get at the cipher-document till he regained his rooms. Merely as a book, the thing seemed to lack thrill. It seemed hours before he reached the dormy-house, and yet Gordon had not returned. So much the better; he would be able to work out the fateful message by himself. It could not be a coincidence, though it had been a long shot to start with. A book of that length (so he had argued to himself) would have been the sort of book one reads in the train. Brotherhood would arrange to have a cipher-message sent him out of the book which he had constantly in his hands at the moment. He would be travelling with it; it was not on the body or by the side of the line; the murderer might not have thought of removing it. This, then, must be the book itself.

As he worked out the message he became less confident. It appeared to run as follows: "Hold and it thoughts with the I highest and to."

"Damn," said Mordaunt Reeves.

CHAPTER VI

THE MOVEMENTS OF MR. DAVENANT

GORDON felt that he was in a favourable position for inquiring into the whereabouts of the mysterious Mr. Davenant. He was himself little known at Paston Whitchurch, since he had only been a month at the dormy-house, and his walks abroad had not carried him much farther than the links. On the other hand, he knew a good deal, from club gossip, about the habits of Mr. Davenant. The Hatcheries was not one of the red-tile-and-rough-cast monuments with which a modern architect had improved the scenery in the neighbourhood of the links; it was a substantial cottage where, in grander days, the home fisherman of Paston Oatvile Park used to live, and look after all that was liquid in the property. It was now occupied permanently by a morose gentleman called Sullivan, who acted as green-keeper to the Club and did a little market gardening at home, and occasionally (that is, during the week-ends) by the scratch player and mystery man, Mr. Davenant. Legally speaking, the cottage was Davenant's property and Sullivan was the caretaker; actually, it would be a clearer account of the position to say that Sullivan rented the cottage from Davenant, and Davenant, every week-end, became the lodger of his own tenant.

It was, then, as a member of the Club that Gordon must approach his interview with Mr. Sullivan, and he was not left much choice of disguises or of excuses. He decided that on the whole bluff would pay best. Accordingly, as soon as Sullivan opened the door in answer to his ring, he began:

"Did Mr. Davenant leave any message for me this morning before he left?"

"What's that?"

"I met Mr. Davenant yesterday on the platform, and tried to make some arrangements with him about having a game next Sunday, and he said he'd leave a note for me at the dormy-house, but it isn't there, so I thought perhaps he'd left it here instead. Did be say anything to you about it?"

"He did not. It's not since Monday morning I've set eyes on Mr. Davenant."

"But he was here yesterday, surely?"

"He was not."

"That's very extraordinary, because I met him on the train, and I certainly understood him to say he was coming here. Could he possibly have been staying at the Club-house?"

"He might."

"Well, I'm sorry to have troubled you. Good evening."

Gordon had the definite impression that when Sullivan

came to the door he was not simply answering the bell; there had been no time for him to hear the bell—he had been going out anyhow. There was a thick hedge at the end of the path which led to the Hatcheries; and behind this hedge, I am sorry to say, Gordon concealed himself. He was the most placid and regular of men, but the ardour of the hunt was beginning to lay hold of him. It was only about a minute and a half later that Sullivan came out, carrying a small bag, and took the path that led to the links. For a moment the watcher thought of shadowing him, then decided that it would be silly. If he went over the golf-links, the open ground would make it quite impossible to follow without being noticed; besides, the links would be full of people whom he knew, and he might easily get delayed. He resolved suddenly on a still more heroic course. Nobody else lived in the cottage— why not try to force an entrance while Sullivan was out, and satisfy himself on circumstantial evidence whether Davenant had really been in the cottage or not?

Breaking into a house is, as a rule, a difficult proceeding, even if it is your own and you know the ropes. To break into a stranger's house, when you are not even certain whether a dog is kept; is a still more heroic affair. The door had locked itself; the ground-floor windows were shut and snibbed. The only chance seemed to be crawling up the roof of a little outhouse and through an open window on the first floor; a bathroom window, to judge by the ample sponge which was drying on the sill. With rubber on his shoes, Gordon made a fairly good job of the outhouse roof. The window was a more serious proposition; it was very narrow, and encumbered on the inside by an array of little bottles. It is easy to put your head and shoulders through such a window, but that means a nose-dive on to the floor. To put your legs through first is to court the possibility of promiscuous breakage. Very carefully Gordon removed all fragile objects out of range, and then with extreme discomfort squeezed his legs through the opening. Even so, there was a moment at which he felt his back must necessarily break, when he was just half-way through. Landing at last without misfortune, he set out quickly on a tour of the silent cottage.

It was only Davenant's part of the house that interested him—the bathroom, a bedroom, a small dining-room, and a study. They all bore the marks of recent inhabitation; but was this anything to go by? Davenant, in any case, would not be expected back for a week, and Sullivan did not strike Gordon as the kind of man who would be inclined to tidy up on Monday when Friday would do just as well. The bed, indeed, was made; but the grate in the study had not been cleared of cigarette-ends; the dining-room table was bare, but Monday's paper was still lying across a chair, as if thrown down at random. On the whole the evidence pointed to Monday as the day of departure; Monday, not Tuesday, appeared on a tear-off calendar; a letter which had arrived on Monday evening was still waiting in the hall; and there were no clothes left in the dirty-clothes basket. Such an authority did Gordon feel himself to be on the subject of washing since his experiences at Binver that he investigated equally the clothes which had come back from the wash, and the list which accompanied them. And here was a curious phenomenon; the list referred to two collars, two handkerchiefs, and a pair of socks as having been disgorged by the Binver authorities, but none of these seemed to have crystallized in real life. "Binver is doing itself proud," murmured Gordon to himself, "or could it possibly be——" He went and looked in the bathroom again: there was the sponge all right, which seemed to insist that Davenant kept a duplicate series of what the shops call toilet accessories; but where was the razor, the shaving soap, the tooth-brush? It seemed, after all, as if Davenant had packed for the week instead of leaving a duplicate week-end set behind him. But—Good Lord! This was still more curious. There was no soap in the bathroom, although there were traces of its presence still discernible. Surely no one packing after a week-end in the country took the soap with him? The face-towel, too, was gone; yet the face-towel was distinctly mentioned in the washing-list. No, decidedly there was something wrong about Davenant's exit.

Another curious thing—there was every evidence that Davenant was a smoker, and yet not a cigarette, not a pipe, not an ounce of tobacco left in the study. Of course,

it was possible that Sullivan was very tidy and put them
away somewhere, or that he was dishonest, and treated
them as perquisites. But once more Gordon had the
impression that Davenant had packed like a man who is
leaving his base, not like a man who has just week-ended
at a Saturday-to-Monday cottage. Like a man going
abroad, even, or why did he take the soap with him?
One piece of supplementary evidence was to be found
in the study. A large and highly ornamented photograph
frame stood on the writing-table there; but it had no
photograph in it, and the back was unfastened, as if the
portrait had been recently and suddenly removed. If
circumstantial evidence went for anything, it seemed
clear that when Davenant left the house last—apparently
on Monday—he left it in the spirit of a man who does
not expect to return immediately, and carries all his
immediate needs with him.

So far the investigation had proceeded, when Gordon
happened to look out of a front window, and was
discomposed by observing that Sullivan was coming back
already down the lane. There was no time to be lost; he
hastily ran downstairs and out at the front door. It would
be taking a considerable risk to trust to the mazes of the
back garden, and he decided to make for the hedge. But
before he could reach it, Sullivan turned the corner into
the garden-path and confronted him.

"I'm so sorry," he said, on the inspiration of the
moment, "but could you tell me what Mr. Davenant's

address is? I shall have to write to him, and this is the only address they've got up at the Club."

"Mr. Davenant left no address," said Sullivan, and, try as he would, Gordon could not determine whether there was suspicion in his tone. However, the awkward corner was turned, and it was with some feeling of self-congratulation that he made his way back to the dormy-house.

He came back to find Reeves closeted with Marryatt and Carmichael, to whom he was explaining the whole story of their adventures. "I hope you won't think it a breach of confidence," was his explanation, "but the last disappointment I've had has made me feel that we must be on the wrong tack somewhere; and it's no good for us two to try and correct each other. It's like correcting the proofs of a book; you must get an outsider in to do it. So I thought, as Marryatt and Carmichael were with us at the start, it would be best to take them fully into our confidence, and make a foursome of it."

"Delighted," said Gordon. "I've been prospecting a bit, but I can't say I've got much forrarder."

"Did you ask whether Davenant was there yesterday?"

"Yes, I interviewed Sullivan on the subject, and he said 'No.'"

"That I can't believe," said Carmichael.

"Why, what about it?" asked Gordon, a little ruffled.

"I'm sure Sullivan didn't say 'No.' Have you never

observed that an Irishman is incapable of saying yes or no to a plain question? If you say, Has the rain stopped, he won't say Yes, or No; he'll say, It has, or It hasn't. The explanation of that is a perfectly simple one: there is no native word for either in Irish, any more than there is in Latin. And that in its turn throws a very important light on the Irish character——"

"Oh, go and throw an important light on your grandmother's ducks," said Reeves. "I want to hear about this interview. Was he telling the truth, d'you think?"

"From his manner, I thought not. So, when his back was turned, I made bold to enter the house and take a look round for myself." And he described the evening's entertainment in detail.

"By Jove, you are warming to the part," said Marryatt. "I should like to see you get run in by the police, Gordon."

"You say," Reeves interrupted, "that you don't think he was there yesterday, on the Tuesday, that is, because he hadn't taken the letter away. He went off, then, on Monday, but when he went off he took with him all that a man normally takes with him if he's going to sleep in a different house that night, plus a piece of soap and a towel, which are not things one usually carries about in one's luggage?"

"That's the best I can make of it," said Gordon.

"And the photograph—it might be an accident, of course, but I feel convinced that he put that in his luggage at the last moment."

"And that's frightfully important," said Reeves, "because it obviously means that on Monday, before anything happened to Brotherhood, Davenant was reckoning on leaving home for some little time; and not returning immediately to wherever it is he lives ordinarily, because he must keep collars and things there. But he also thought he might be away for some longish time, or he wouldn't have worried to take the photograph with him. What was the frame like?"

"Quite modern; no maker's name on it."

"I'm afraid that means the murder must have been a premeditated one," put in Marryatt. "I hope it's not uncharitable to say so, but I never did like Davenant. I don't think I'm ordinarily a person of very narrow religious views, and I've known Romans that were quite easy to get on with. But Davenant was a person of quite ungovernable temper, you must remember that."

"His ungovernable temper would be much more important," objected Gordon, "if the murder were not a premeditated one."

"But it's not only that," persisted Marryatt. "To me, there was always something sinister about him; he had fits of melancholy, and would rail at the people and the politicians he didn't like in a way that was almost frightening. Surely I'm not alone in that impression?"

"What did Davenant look like?" asked Carmichael suddenly.

"Good Lord," said Reeves, "you ought to remember

that well enough. You must have met him down here pretty well every week-end, and he was quite well known."

"Oh yes," explained Carmichael. "I know what he looked like. I'm only asking you to see if *you* remember. If you were asked in a witness-box, what would you say Davenant looked like?"

"Well," said Reeves, rather taken aback, "I suppose one would certainly say he was very dark. Very dark hair, I mean, and a great deal of it, so that it made the rest of his face rather unnoticeable. What I generally notice about a man is his eyes, and I never got much impression of Davenant's, because he nearly always wore those heavy horn-rimmed spectacles. And then of course he was a rattling good player. If he murdered Brotherhood, as Marryatt seems positive he did, I can tell you one motive that I can't accept for his doing it. He wasn't jealous of Brotherhood's golf. Poor old Brotherhood was about as rotten as Davenant is good."

"It's very extraordinary to me," said Carmichael, "that you should say all that, and yet not have arrived at the obvious fact about this mystery. The root fact, I mean, which you have to take into account before you start investigating the circumstances at all. You simply haven't seen that fact, although it's right under your nose. And that's a very curious thing, the way you can look at a complex of facts ninety-nine times, and only notice the point of them the hundredth time. The phenomenon of attention——"

"Oh, cut it out," said Gordon; "what is the fact we haven't noticed?"

"Oh, that," said Carmichael lightly, "merely that Brotherhood is Davenant, and Davenant is Brotherhood."

CHAPTER VII

CARMICHAEL'S ACCOUNT OF IT

"GOOD Lord," said Reeves, when the first shock of astonishment was over, "tell us some more about it. How did you know?"

Carmichael joined the tips of his fingers and beamed at them, secure of an audience at last. "Well, you've just admitted that all you can remember about Davenant is hair and spectacles. That is, his disguise. Of course the man wore a wig. He was a fictitious personality from start to finish."

"Except for his golf," suggested Gordon.

"Yes, that was real enough; but Brotherhood's wasn't. Don't you see that the two characters are complementary, suspiciously complementary? Brotherhood is here all the week, but never during the week-ends; Davenant is only seen from Saturday to Monday. Davenant is Catholic, so as to be violently distinguished from the atheist Brotherhood. Davenant is good at golf; so Brotherhood has to be distinguished by being very bad at golf, and that, to me, is the mystery of the whole concern. How a scratch player could have the iron self-control to play that rotten game all the week, merely to prevent our suspecting his identity, beats me entirely. And yet you could find parallel instances; old Lord Mersingham, for example——"

"Do you mean," said Gordon in a shocked voice, "that Brotherhood pulled his drives like that on purpose?"

"Precisely. After all, don't you remember that day, let me see, I think it was last February, when Brotherhood played for fifty pounds, and went round in eighty-nine? Of course, there are flukes even in golf. I remember myself——"

"Well," said Gordon, "I think the Committee ought to do something about it. Dash it all, I was his partner in the foursomes."

"De mortuis," suggested Reeves. "But I still don't see why he wanted to do it, I'm afraid. Why, the thing's been going on for years."

"Well, none of us know much about Brotherhood's business; but I gather from what people are saying about the bankruptcy that it was a pretty shady one. They haven't traced any hole in the accounts; but if there ever was a man you would expect to go bankrupt and then skip (I believe it is called) with what is described in such circumstance as the boodle, that man was Brotherhood. He foresaw the probability of this for years, and made very careful and subtle preparations for meeting the situation. The important thing on such occasions is to have an *alter ego*. The difficulty is to establish an *alter ego* on the spur of the moment. Brotherhood knew better. He had been working up his *alter ego* for years."

"Right under our noses!" protested Reeves.

"That was the cleverness of it," said Carmichael. "If there was a Mr. Brotherhood at Paston Oatvile, and a Mr. Davenant every week-end at Brighton, nobody would be deceived; it's a stale old dodge to keep up a double establishment in two different places. The genius of Brotherhood's invention was that he kept up two establishments within a stone's throw of each other. Nobody here could actually say that he'd seen Brotherhood and Davenant together, that goes without saying. But the two personalities were real personalities in the same world; and there were hosts of witnesses who would declare that they knew both. If Brotherhood suddenly ceased to exist, the last place where anybody would thing of looking for him would be the house next door."

"Good God, what a fool I've been!" said Mordaunt Reeves.

"The separate banking-account would be particularly useful to such a man," Carmichael went on. "If we could find out where Davenant banked, I have no doubt that we should discover a substantial balance. But of course, he wouldn't bank here."

"Why not?" asked Gordon.

"Because Brotherhood would want to deal with the local bank, and it's a very unsafe business making your signature in a forged writing. So Davenant will have banked in London. By the way, that's another point, did you notice that Davenant always used a typewriter? He couldn't risk the use of a false handwriting."

"Elementary, my dear Watson," murmured Gordon to himself.

"Well, he knew when the crash was coming; it was all carefully prearranged. He had even the impudence to book a sleeping car to Glasgow."

"But that's a difficulty, surely," put in Reeves. "Because he ordered the sleeper not as Davenant but as Brotherhood. Now, you make out that Brotherhood was to have disappeared, as from yesterday, and Davenant was to have become a permanency. Why didn't he order a sleeper in the name of Davenant?"

"How often am I to tell you, my dear Reeves, that you are dealing with a genius? If Davenant had ordered a sleeper just at that moment, attention might have been directed to him. But ordering a sleeper for Brotherhood would merely strengthen the impression that Brotherhood had disappeared. If that was all—personally I believe the scheme was even more audacious. I believe Davenant did mean to go away, for a time at any rate, and by that very train. He would join it at Crewe, travelling in an ordinary first-class carriage. Then at Wigan—bless my soul!"

"What's the matter?" asked Gordon.

"I find myself unaccountably unable to recollect

whether the 7.30 from Euston stops at Wigan. However, it will do for the sake of argument.

"At Wigan an anonymous passenger, Davenant, of course, would ask the sleeping-car attendant whether he had a vacant berth. And the man was bound to have a vacant berth—Brotherhood's. There was one person in the world whom nobody would suspect of being Brotherhood—the stranger who had been accommodated, quite accidentally, with Brotherhood's berth."

"It's wonderful!" said Marryatt.

"But of course, all that is only speculation. Now we come to something of which we can give a more accurate account—the plans which this Brotherhood-Davenant made for the act of metamorphosis. I take it this was his difficulty—Brotherhood and Davenant (naturally enough) do not know one another. If Davenant walks out of Brotherhood's office in London, it will create suspicion—the change, then, must not happen in London. If Davenant is suddenly seen walking out of Brotherhood's bungalow, that again will create suspicion; the change, then, must not take place at Paston Whitchurch. The thing must be managed actually on the journey between the two places. That is why Brotherhood-Davenant wears such very non-committal clothes—hosiery by which, in case of accident, he cannot be traced; the very handkerchief he takes with him is one belonging to a stranger, which has come into his possession by accident. He even has two watches, one to suit either character. Thus, you see, he can be Brotherhood or Davenant at will, by slipping on a wig and a pair of spectacles.

"He did not do anything so crude as to change once for all, suddenly, from Brotherhood to Davenant at a given point on his journey. He alternated between the two rôles all along the line—I have always wondered what is the origin of that curious phrase 'all along the line'; here I use it, you will understand, in a quite literal sense. Davenant got out at Paston Oatvile—the porter saw him. But, as we now know, it must have been Brotherhood who was travelling in the 4.50 from Paston Oatvile on. Yet it was as Davenant that he would have got out at Paston Whitchurch."

"How do you know that?" asked Reeves.

"The ticket, of course. Brotherhood had a season, naturally, for he went up and down every day. At Paston Whitchurch, therefore, Brotherhood would have produced a season. It was Davenant who needed an ordinary single. The effect of all this was to create the simultaneous impression that both Brotherhood and Davenant came back to Paston Whitchurch that afternoon, and came by the same train. There was only one hitch in the plan, which could hardly have been foreseen. If Brotherhood happened to be murdered on the way, it would look very much as if Davenant had murdered him. And unfortunately he was murdered."

"Then you don't think it was suicide?" asked Marryatt, with a catch in his voice.

"If it was suicide, it was the result of a momentary insanity, almost incredibly sudden in its incidence. Suicide was certainly not part of the plan. A bogus suicide was, of course, a conceivable expedient; it would have been one way of getting rid of the undesirable Brotherhood's existence. But consider what that means. It means getting hold of a substitute who looked exactly like Brotherhood—he could not foresee the excoriation of the features—and murdering him at unawares. It meant, further, that Davenant would be suspected of the murder. No plan could have been more difficult or more clumsy."

"Then you mean," said Marryatt, "that we have to look for a murderer, somebody quite unknown to us?"

"I didn't say that," replied Carmichael, with a curious look. "I mean that we have to look for a murderer, some one whom we have not hitherto suspected. If Davenant murdered Brotherhood, that was certainly suicide; for Davenant was Brotherhood. But that seems to me impossible. The evidence all goes to show that there was a very careful plot in contemplation, which was cut short by a quite unforeseen counterplot."

"But look here," said Reeves, "if the original plan had come off, did he mean to come back here and live on here as Davenant?"

"You mustn't expect me to know everything; I can

only go by the indications. But I should say that he really would have come back here as Davenant, perhaps about three weeks later, and settled down permanently at the Hatcheries; or perhaps even—he was a very remarkable man—he would have bought up Brotherhood's bungalow. You see, he liked the place; he liked the company; the only thing he disliked was having to play golf badly, and that necessity disappeared, once he settled down as Davenant. A wig is a nuisance, but so is baldness. The last place where anybody would look for Mr. Brotherhood, last heard of on the way to Glasgow, would be Paston Whitchurch, where Mr. Brotherhood had lived."

"I'm afraid I'm very stupid," said Gordon, "one of Nature's Watsons, as I said yesterday. But what about all the silly little indications I found at the Hatcheries an hour ago? Do they back up your theory, or are they wide of the mark?"

"It's all according to schedule," explained Carmichael, "but for a reason quite different from any you imagined. You must consider that the things we really find it hard to change are not the important things of life, our moral or religious or political standpoint, but our common, daily habits of living. Brotherhood might be an atheist, and Davenant a Catholic; Brotherhood a violent Radical, Davenant a Diehard Tory. But every man has his own preference in razors and in shaving-soap and in tooth-powder; and if you looked into the thing, you would find that if Davenant used A's shaving-soap, so did Brotherhood; if Brotherhood used B's tooth-powder, so did Davenant. There lay the real danger of detection. There was just the danger that somebody— shall we say, an interfering old don?—might hit upon the truth of the secret, and make investigations. Accordingly, those little traces must be obliterated. And they have been, for Davenant was careful to take them away with him. And so has the photograph, a photograph which, I suspect, had a duplicate in Brotherhood's house—you see, neither Brotherhood nor Davenant could live without it."

"But the collars and the socks? Surely nobody is so intimately wedded to one particular type of collar——"

"A blind. Davenant was to look as if he were packing up to go away, so he must take some clothes with him, not merely the shaving things."

"But the towel and the soap? Surely they were not necessary to complete the illusion?"

"No, they are even more significant. Davenant—don't you remember?—had rather darker eyebrows than Brotherhood. Quite easily done, of course, with paint. But you want something to wash it off with; and there are no corridors on the slow trains."

"Yes, but look here," objected Reeves, "why did he want to take all these things away with him on Monday?—it was on Tuesday he was timed to disappear—or rather, actually on Wednesday: his sleeper was for Wednesday."

"I don't think he meant to sleep the Tuesday night at the Hatcheries. He had transferred his base somewhere else—to London, I suppose—and his visit to Paston Whitchurch, on the pretext of picking up something he had left behind, was merely meant to establish, in our eyes, the fact that he was a different man from Brotherhood."

"There's one more thing, though," said Marryatt; "I'm afraid it's a kind of professional objection. Is it possible that a man who was really an atheist would be at the pains to go over every Sunday to Mass at Paston Bridge? Davenant, you see, was very regular about that. Or, granted that he was really a Catholic, could he bring himself to get up and preach atheist doctrines on the village green?"

Carmichael pulled a wry face. "I'm afraid, Marryatt, you are altogether too confiding. Don't you see that he was a Catholic, and was doing the work of his own Church by turning the villagers against you and your doctrines? Don't you see that if he managed to make atheists of your people, it would be all the easier for the priest at Paston Bridge to make Romans of them?"

"In fact," said Gordon, "what it comes to is this: we have got to look for a criminal still; but it's no use looking for Davenant?"

"You would be chasing a phantom," said Carmichael.

CHAPTER VIII

THE INQUEST, AND A FRESH CLUE

THE inquest was held on the following afternoon (that is, the afternoon of Thursday) in the village school at Paston Whitchurch. As he sat waiting to give his evidence, Reeves found his mind dominated, as the mind is dominated at such moments, almost entirely by irrelevant sense-impressions. There was the curious smell of the schoolroom, which always suggests (it is hard to know why) ink and chalk. There was the irritating pant and hoot of motors and motor-bicycles outside the open windows. There was the inevitable series of animals represented round the walls, looking like the religious emblems of some strange, totemistic worship. The one opposite Reeves had a caption underneath it in very large letters, THE PIG IS A MAMMAL, as if to clear up any possible doubts which might be felt by the youth of the parish as to what a pig was. There were the names cut and inked on the desks; especially intriguing was the signature of "H. Precious"—how did people in the country get such odd names? And why were there so few names like that in the London Telephone Directory? Carmichael would probably have a theory about this. . . .

Such were the thoughts that kept dawdling through his mind, when he felt that he ought to be forming important decisions. What was he going to say when he was called in evidence? Was he going to give any hint as to his suspicions of foul play, or would it be better to leave the police to their own unaided intelligence? And if he did breathe his suspicions, was he bound to mention the golf-ball which he had found at the top of the embankment? Would they ask how he had employed his time between the moment when he found the body and the moment when the police arrived? He wished that he had discussed all this beforehand with Gordon—or would that have been conspiring to defeat the ends of justice? Anyhow, he wished the preliminary proceedings would hurry up.

When he was actually called, he found that he was not asked for his opinion on any theoretical point, and indeed was given no opportunity of getting a word in edgeways as to the view he had formed of the case. He was only asked details about the exact time of his discovery (this question confused him rather) and the precise attitude in which the body lay. Instead of being criticized for disturbing the clues by removing the dead body, he was thanked for having removed it. Altogether, the proceedings struck him as singularly ill-calculated to assist in the clearing up of a mystery. It seemed rather as if Society were performing a solemn act of purification over the remains of the dead. In the end he sat down feeling exactly (the atmosphere helped) as if he were back at school again, had just been "put on construing," not at the passage he had specially "mugged up," but at the passage next door to it, and had acquitted himself better than he expected in the circumstances. The feeling was intensified when Marryatt got up; Marryatt was still intensely nervous over the prospect of a suicide verdict; and he answered the questions put to him confusedly and at random, like a schoolboy who has omitted the formality of preparing the lesson at all.

The heroine of the afternoon was undoubtedly Mrs. Bramston. The coroner was not ready for her, and she got right in under his guard, pouring out a flood of promiscuous information which he neither demanded nor desired. Then strangers came—people from Brotherhood's office in London, people from the Insurance Company, people representing the creditors: people, too, who represented the railway company, and dilated for hours on the impossibility of falling out of their trains by accident. In fact, nobody seemed to care a straw about the mangled temple of humanity that lay in the next room, or whether it cried to heaven for vengeance. Only two points mattered, whether the Insurance Company had got to pay up, and whether the Railway Company owed Compensation. Brotherhood had, as far as could be discovered, neither kith nor kin in the world, and it was perhaps not unnatural that the verdict given was one of death by suicide. Yet Marryatt was to be freed of his apprehensions: Brotherhood had looked worried lately at the office—had said, "Damn you, get out of the way" to the lift-boy—had complained of headaches. He had committed suicide, clearly while of unsound mind; and Marryatt might get on with the funeral.

Marryatt seemed five years younger when they met afterwards to discuss the situation. Strange, Reeves reflected, how in certain natures the wish is father to the thought. Only last night Marryatt had seemed eager to follow up the clues of a murder, so as to get the bugbear of suicide off his mind; now that the act of suicide was declared inculpable, he showed no great interest in prosecuting the inquiry. "It's a mystery," he kept on saying, "and I don't think we're ever likely to get to the bottom of it. If we could have hunted Davenant, we should have had something to go on. Now that we know Davenant was a fictitious personage, what's the use of worrying? We've no clues that can help us to any further action. Unless, of course, you like to go to the police and tell them what you know."

But to this Reeves would not consent. Ever since the apparent indifference with which the police had treated his warning chits when he was in the Military Intelligence, he had longed for an opportunity to show them in the wrong.

"There are one or two things," he pointed out, "which we've still got to account for. There's that cipher message we found in Brotherhood's pocket. There's the list we found on the back of it; only four words, but full of suggestion. And there's the golf ball we found on the embankment—there we have the actual clue in our pockets."

"A precious poor sort of clue," objected Gordon. "Leave that ball lying about, and every third man in the club will be prepared to adopt it as his long-lost property."

Carmichael seemed destined to overwhelm them with surprises. At this point he suddenly remarked, "You know, that's not all the clues we've got. There's one that dropped out of poor Brotherhood's pocket as the caddies were carrying off the body to the tool-house. At least, the caddies said so: my private impression is that the young ruffians searched the pockets on their own—"

"Why on earth should they do that?" asked Reeves.

"Well, you know what caddies are—it's a demoralizing profession. Not that I believe much in boys going to school myself, but it does keep them out of mischief. Those two boys, I think, went through the pockets on their own."

"They left four bob there," suggested Gordon.

"Yes, boys are frightened of stealing money; they connect it with going to prison. But they don't mind stealing other things; I think they could tell you why the pouch was empty, and why there was only one cigarette left in the case—they were too clever to clear both completely. After all, you know, it isn't very long since people gave up 'wrecking' in Cornwall. I remember a very interesting conversation I had with a man down there in the *Lugger* Inn at Fowey——"

"You were going to tell us something about a clue," said Gordon gently.

"Ah yes: one of them came up to me afterwards—it was the one they call Ginger. I wonder why are boys with red hair called Ginger? Ginger is of a greenish-yellow tinge, if you come to think of it. Where was I? Yes, he came up to me with a photograph, and told me that it had fallen out of one of the pockets as they carried the body. That is almost impossible, you know, for a man always carries photographs in his breast pocket, and a thing can't fall out of a man's breast pocket unless you turn him upside down and shake him. Ginger was obviously scared at the thought that he might be concealing a clue—he referred to it as a 'clue' himself—and did not care to give it to the police; so he handed it over to me."

"And you?"

"I have it here in my pocket—the breast pocket, observe. To tell the truth, I am a little absentminded, and it was only during the inquest that I remembered the photograph; it seemed to me too late then to mention anything about it in public."

"Carmichael," said Gordon very seriously, "if you don't produce that photograph it will, I gather, be necessary to turn you upside down and shake you."

"Of course, of course." Carmichael fumbled in his pocket, and from a voluminous pocket-book produced with great deliberation the object of their impatience. It represented the head and shoulders of a young woman: the features were refined, and might in real life have been beautiful. The camera cannot lie, but the camera of the local "artist" generally finds it difficult to tell nothing but the truth: and this was the work of a Mr. Campbell, whose studio was no further off than Binver. Meanwhile the photograph was not in its first youth; and the style of coiffure represented suggested (with what could be seen of the dress) a period dating some ten years back. It was not signed or initialled anywhere.

"Well," said Reeves, when the trove had been handed round, "that doesn't prove that we're much further on. But it looks as if we had come across a phase of Brotherhood's life that wasn't alluded to at the inquest."

Gordon shuddered. "Just think if one went off the hooks suddenly, and people came round and tried to dig up one's past from the old photographs and keepsakes one had hidden away in drawers! One should destroy everything—certainly one should destroy everything."

But Reeves was no sentimentalist; he was a sleuth-hound with nose down on the trail. "Let's see," he reflected, "I can't remember at the moment what the present Binver photographer is called."

"You will find it," suggested Carmichael, "on that group over your head." Reeves had it down in a minute.

"Yes, that's right: Campbell," he said. "Now, if one of us goes off in Binver and says he's found this photograph, and would Mr. Campbell be kind enough to let us know the address it was originally sent to, so that we can restore it, that ought to do the trick. Photographers are full of professional etiquette, but I don't see that we could go wrong here."

"I don't mind going," said Marryatt; "as a matter of fact, I've got to ride in to see a man on business."

"Heaven defend me," said Reeves, "from having business with anybody at Binver!"

"You will, though, with this man, some day."

"Why, who is it?"

"The undertaker," said Marryatt.

"Undertakers," said Carmichael, "have been very much maligned in literature. They are always represented as either cynical or morbid in the exercise of their profession. As a matter of fact, I am told that no class of men is more considerate or more tactful."

"I'll be back in three-quarters of an hour," said Marryatt, buttoning the photograph away. "Carmichael, I hope you won't produce any more clues while I'm away."

When Marryatt had gone, and Carmichael had sauntered off to the billiard-room, Reeves sat on there fidgeting and discussing the possible significance of the latest find.

"It's odd," he said, "how one can live for years in the

artificial life of a club like this and not know one's
neighbours in the least. We're a world to ourselves, and
an outside face like that conveys nothing to us; probably
the name won't either. What beats me at present about
the photograph is this—how long ago would you say
that photograph was taken?"

"I'm not an authority on ladies' fashions, I'm afraid,
but surely it's pre-war."

"Exactly. Now, Brotherhood only came here just at
the end of the war, at least, he only joined the Club then;
I asked the Secretary about it. And 'Davenant' joined
even later, only a year or two ago. When a man takes a
house here, one assumes that he's only come here for
the golf. But it looks as if Brotherhood, or else his
phantom self, Davenant, knew the Binver world
already—at least well enough to possess photographs
of its belles."

"Not necessarily," Gordon pointed out. "She may have
had no later portrait to give him than that one, even if
she gave it him only a year or two ago."

"That's true. And yet women generally keep their
portraits pretty well up-to-date. Here's another point—
from the caddie's account, it seems that this portrait must
have been loose in the pocket; but he can't always have
carried it like that. . . . Good Lord, what a fool I am!
What size was the empty frame in Davenant's cottage?"

"Oh, just that size. It's a common size, of course, but
I suppose most likely it was that portrait which

'Davenant' caught up in a hurry before he left his house; and crammed it into his pocket anyhow. Assuming, of course, that Carmichael's right."

"Yes, that makes the thing as clear as daylight, so far. I hope Marryatt makes good time. Look how slow we've been on the murderer's tracks; we've given him two full days already."

"By the way," said Gordon, "I've just remembered— Thursday's early closing day at Binver."

CHAPTER IX

THE ANIMATED PICTURE

"WELL," said Reeves impatiently, as Marryatt came, rather late, into the dining-room, "did you find out?"

"Yes, I went round to Campbell's——"

"But it's early closing day."

"Yes, only . . . only Campbell was open, for some reason. He made no difficulty about identifying the portrait or about giving me the address. When he told me the name and address I remembered quite a lot about her."

"Who is she, then?"

"Her name is Miss Rendall-Smith. Her father, old Canon Rendall-Smith, was Rector of Binver for a long time, a learned old man, I believe, but rather a bore. He died some years before the war—I should think it would be about 1910, and left her very badly off; she left the neighbourhood then—that was just before I came. Some time during the early part of the war she came back, apparently in much better circumstances, for she took that old brick house with the white window-frames that stands next the Church and looks as if it was the Rectory but isn't. She lives there still; she did a good deal of public work during the war, subscriptions and things, but I never actually came across her. She's a fine-looking woman still, Campbell told me—by the way, there was no reticence about Campbell. He showed me a more recent portrait of her which he was very proud of, and told me he thought it was a pity a lady like that didn't marry. Altogether, we seem to have struck a public character, and a very good woman, by all that's said of her."

"H'm," said Reeves, "and Brotherhood kept a portrait of her—or rather, Brotherhood in his capacity as Davenant kept a portrait of her, and took it away with him when he meant to leave these parts for a bit. It seems to me she ought to be able to tell us something about him."

"Good Lord!" said Marryatt, "you aren't going to introduce yourself to *her* as the *Daily Mail* reporter? Hang it all, it's one thing to take in Mrs. Bramston—"

"And another thing to take in Miss Rendall-Smith, because she's a lady? I'm afraid that seems to me mere sentimentalism."

"What I meant was, if you present yourself to Miss Rendall-Smith as a reporter, she'll turn you out of the house."

"Ye-es. There's something in that. But then, I wouldn't say I'd come from the *Daily Mail;* I'd say I'd come from the *County Herald*, and that I was commissioned to do a write-up of Brotherhood as a prominent local personage."

"But how," objected Carmichael, "would you explain the fact that you were coming to her? Remember, it isn't certain that she knew Brotherhood at all, that is, in his own person. You see it was not to Brotherhood but to Davenant that she gave the photograph. And natural enough—if I had been in that position, I would sooner have gone courting as Davenant than as Brotherhood."

"I could simply pretend I was coming to her as to one of the oldest residents."

"Tactful Openings, Number One," suggested Gordon, crumbling his bread. "No, Reeves, it won't do. I'd like to see you dressed up as a reporter again, because I think there's something very fetching about it. But I don't believe that even in that disguise you will win the heart of a mature female. You'll have to think out some other dodge."

"I suppose you'd like me to burgle her house while she's out," said Reeves, with unnecessary irritation.

"But you don't want to see her house," objected the literal-minded Gordon, "you want to see her."

"Very well, then," said Reeves, "I shall go and tell her the truth. At least, I shall tell her that we're investigating Brotherhood's murder, and that this portrait of her was found on the body. I shall urge her to tell me if she knows of any enemies that Brotherhood had, any secrets which might throw light upon his end."

"That's far the best principle," agreed Gordon.

"Always tell the truth, and people will never believe you."

"Why shouldn't she believe me?"

"No reason in the world; only as a matter of fact she won't. It's rather a satire on humanity, but I've always found that the safest way to conceal a fact is to state it quite baldly. Then people always think you're pulling their legs, or being sarcastic, and the secret is preserved."

"You're a sceptical old Sadducee. I don't believe a woman like this would have such a low view of humanity."

"Like what?"

"Like the portrait."

"Are you falling in love with her already? Marryatt, it seems to me, between funerals and marriages, you're going to be a busy man."

"Don't be a fool," said Reeves. "I don't know anything about women, except that some of them are so ugly I recognize them when I meet them in the street. This clearly isn't one of them. But I have trained myself to judge faces a bit, and this looks to me like the face of a woman who's straight herself and expects others to be straight with her."

"Let's have another look," urged Gordon. Marryatt produced the photograph, and it was passed round once more. "I dare say you're right," admitted Gordon. "The curious thing to me is that a good-looking woman like that who's not actually a beauty—not classic features, I mean—should look so deadly serious when she's having her photograph taken. I should have thought even Mr. Campbell would have had the sense to make a little photographer's joke; or at least tell her to moisten her lips."

"You're right," said Carmichael. "The look is a very serious one; but I believe a portrait is all the better for that—as a portrait, I mean. Have you ever thought what an advantage the historians of the future will have over us? Think how late portraiture itself comes into history; I think I'm right in saying that a thumb-nail sketch of Edward II in the margin of an old chronicle is the earliest portrait preserved to us in English history. And when portrait-painting did come in, how soon the art was corrupted! You can see that Holbein was telling the truth; but by the time you get to Vandyck it's all court flattery. Whereas the historians of the future will be able to see what we really were like."

"It looks to me," said Reeves, "a sad face—the face of a woman who's had a good deal of trouble. I feel somehow that the serious pose of the mouth was natural to her."

"I don't think that's the ordinary impression you'd get from her face," put in Marryatt.

"How on earth do you know?" asked Reeves, staring.

"Well, you see, Campbell showed me this later photograph of her, and it wasn't at all like that."

"Well," suggested Gordon, "it's not much good discussing the portrait if Reeves is going to see the lovely original to-morrow. I want to know what's wrong with a game of bridge?"

"Good idea," said Marryatt, "it'll take our minds off the murder. You know, I think you fellows are getting rather fanciful about the whole thing."

"All right," said Reeves, "my room, though, not downstairs. What's the good of having one's own fireplace if one can't light a fire in October?"

Reeves' room deserves, perhaps, a fuller description than it has hitherto been given. It had been the best bedroom of the old Dower-house, and for some reason had been spared when several smaller rooms had been divided up, at the time of the club's installation. It was, consequently, a quite unspoiled piece of early Tudor architecture; there were latticed windows with deep recesses; dark, irregular beams supported the white-plastered ceiling; the walls were oak-panelled; the fireplace open and of genuine old brick. When the fire, reluctant after long desuetude, had been induced to crackle, and threw flickering reflections where the shade of the electric light gave subdued half tones, there was an air of comfort which seemed to dispel all thought of detective problems, of murderers stalking the world unpunished, of the open grave that waited in Paston Oatvile churchyard.

Gordon put down the photograph on a jutting cornice

that went round the panelling. "There, Reeves," he said, "you shall sit opposite the lady, and derive inspiration from her. I cannot ask you to hope that she will smile upon your efforts, but it ought to be an encouragement."

They were soon immersed in that reverential silence and concentration which the game fosters: and if Miss Rendall-Smith's portrait did not receive much of their attention, it is probable that the lady herself, had she been present, would have been treated with little more ceremony. Reeves, however, was bad at taking his mind off a subject, and when, as dummy, he was given a short interval of unrepose, his eyes strayed to the photograph anew. Was this the face, perhaps, that had lured Brotherhood to his strange doom? Was she even an accomplice, burdened now with the participation of a guilty secret? Or was she the sufferer by the crime; and did she wait vainly for news of Davenant, little knowing that it was Davenant who lay waiting for burial at Paston Whitchurch? Poor woman, it seemed likely in any case that she would have much to bear—was it decent to inflict on her a detective interview and a series of importunate questions? He crushed down the insurgent weakness: there was no other way for it, she must be confronted with the facts. The face looked even more beautiful as you saw it in the firelight, shaded from the glare of the lamp. He strolled over to look at it again just as the last trump was led.

"Good God!"

The others turned, in all the irritation of an interrupted train of thought, to find him staring at the photograph as if in horror. Then he stepped quickly across to the lamp, and turned it sideways so as to throw the light full on the wall. And then they too turned a little pale. The photograph had smiled.

There was, to be sure, only the faintest flicker of a smile on the lips; you could not give any formula of it or trace the lines of it. And yet it was the simultaneous impression of these four men that the whole character, the whole impression of the face before them had changed while they had played three hands of bridge. The whole face was indefinably more human and more beautiful; but you could not say why.

"Oh, for God's sake let's give the beastly thing up!" cried Marryatt. "It doesn't do to meddle with these things; one doesn't know what one's up against. Reeves, I know it hurts your vanity to leave an inquiry half-finished, but I'm sure it's a mistake to go on. Brotherhood, you know—he wasn't quite canny; I always thought there was something uncanny about him. Do let's give it up."

"The thing isn't possible," said Reeves slowly. "It's the difference of the light, I think; the light wasn't so strong downstairs. It's funny how one can imagine these things."

"I was never in a haunted house myself," said Carmichael, "but I remember very well the College used to own land at Luttercombe, where the De Mumfords

lived, don't you know, and our old Bursar always insisted
that he heard screams in the night when he slept there. I
don't believe in these things myself, though; fancy can
play such extraordinary tricks."

"But look here, we all noticed the difference,"
objected Marryatt.

"Well, there is such a thing as collective hallucination.
Somebody tells us the face looks grave, and our
imagination reads gravity into it; and then somebody says
it's changed, and we can't see the gravity there any
longer."

"That's it," said Reeves, who was pouring himself
out a stiff whisky-and-soda. "It's collective hallucination.
Must be."

It was characteristic of Gordon that, without
expressing any opinion, he had been the only one of the
four who quite liked to go up and touch the photograph.
He held it now close under the light, and looked at it
from different angles.

"I'm hanged if it doesn't look different," he said at
last. "Sympathetic ink? No, that's nonsense. But it's a
dashed rum thing, photography: I wonder if the heat of
the room can have brought out some bit of shadow on
the face that wasn't visible before?"

"A damp spot possibly," said Reeves, "which has
faded out. It was rather close to the fire. Oh, what's the
good of worrying? Let's all go to bed. I'm going to lock
the thing up in the drawer here; and we can have another

look at it in the morning. We're all over-excited."

"That's it," said Carmichael, opening the door, "I remember once in Eastern Roumelia——" but, as he managed to fall down the step into the passage, the reminiscence was fortunately lost.

CHAPTER X

IN WHICH A BOOK IS MORE COMMUNICATIVE
THAN A LADY

MORNING, as might have been expected, brought division of counsel. Mordaunt Reeves could now find no difference between the photograph as he saw it at the moment and the photograph as he had seen it at dinner the previous night. Carmichael agreed with him, though he still talked a good deal about collective hallucinations. Gordon could not make up his mind one way or the other; only Marryatt was certain that there had been a change. Anyhow, change or no change, Reeves put the once dreaded object in his pocket, and set out after breakfast in Gordon's side-car. Gordon volunteered to drive him over, though firmly announcing that he would not go inside Miss Rendall-Smith's house; Carmichael sought to deter them by wise saws and modern instances, and they left him *multa volentem dicere* at the clubhouse door.

It must be confessed that Reeves felt a certain misgiving as he waited in Miss Rendall-Smith's drawing-room. Rooms do echo personalities, and this drawing-room spoke of a forceful one; the furnishing was strategically perfect, the flowers were arranged purposefully, the books were books that had been collected, not simply amassed. The room smelt, Reeves said afterwards, of not having been smoked in. Nor did the lady of the house belie this first impression. Her beauty was still undeniable, but it was something more than beauty which disarmed you. You felt at once that she was kind and that she was competent, but you felt that if a choice had to be made she would be competent rather than kind. She might have been the matron of a big hospital, instead of an unoccupied householder in a small country town.

"Good-morning, Mr. Reeves," she said, "it's very kind of you to come and see me. I don't think we ever met, did we? I know the Secretary, of course, and several of the club members, but we're rather out of the golfing world down here. But my maid says you want to see me on urgent business—please tell me if I can be of any use."

Mordaunt Reeves, with an unaccountable feeling of being the detected rather than the detective, produced the photograph from his pocket, and asked melodramatically, "Excuse me, Miss Rendall-Smith, but do you recognize this photograph?"

There was just the fraction of a pause, just the suspicion of a gasp. Then she said, "Of course I do! I don't know whether my looking-glass would, of course . . . but a thing like this can't be done behind one's back, can it? I think it was taken when I was here before, while my father was still alive. What did you want to know about it?"

"I'm afraid it must seem very impertinent of me to be asking questions about it, but the thing is of importance. I think I'd better tell you the whole situation. You'll have heard, of course, this sad news about poor old Brotherhood, at Paston Whitchurch?"

"I read about it, of course, in the paper."

"Well, one or two of his friends, that is, of people who knew him down at the club, aren't quite satisfied with the line the police have taken about it. They think— we think they swallowed the idea of suicide too easily, without examining all the facts; and—well, the thing we can't feel certain of is that there hasn't been foul play."

"Foul play? But why should anybody . . ."

"Oh, we've no suspicion of any motive. We thought, perhaps, that was where you might help us. It was I and some friends of mine who actually found the body, you know, and there were certain indications which suggested to us that Brotherhood had . . . had been murdered. There was the position of his hat, for example—still, we needn't go into all that. We did entertain the suspicion very strongly, only the clues we had at our disposal weren't sufficient to let us follow up our suspicions, if you see what I mean. The only one which we felt might help us to get any further was this photograph. By a mere accident, for which I'm not responsible, it didn't get into the hands of the police."

"The police know nothing about it?"

"We have no reason to think they do. But it was found in Brotherhood's pocket—at least, it was found in circumstances which made it quite clear that it had fallen out of his pocket, when the . . . when his body was being moved."

Miss Rendall-Smith took another look at the portrait, which still lay in her hands. "Then," she said, "what exactly do you want me to do about it?"

"Well, you must understand, of course, that we are very reluctant to open up any subject which may be painful to you. But at the same time, since it seemed likely that you had some knowledge of Brotherhood's history and circumstances which the world at large doesn't share, we thought perhaps you would tell us whether you can form any guess yourself as to the circumstances of his death. To put it in the concrete, do you know of any one who would have a motive for wishing ill to Brotherhood, or who might be likely to take his life?"

"I see. You want me to help justice. But you want me to help you, not the police."

"We are helping the police ourselves. Only the police are not always very—what shall I say?—the police don't always encourage help from outside; there is a good deal of red tape about their methods. I was in the Military Intelligence myself during the war, and had some opportunity of seeing the unfortunate effects of rivalry and jealousy between the various departments. We have not approached the police; we thought it best to work on our own until we could present them with a *fait accompli*. That is why we have not even mentioned to the police the existence of this photograph which we found on the body."

"Mr. Reeves———"

A woman can use a surname as a bludgeon. That title of respect, "Mr. So-and-So," which expresses our relations to the outside world, has often, indeed, had an ominous ring for us. Deans used it when they were protesting at our neglect of chapels; proctors, when they urged the immodesty of going out to dinner without a cap and gown. But nobody can use it with the same annihilating effect as a woman scorned. "Mister"—you are a man, I a defenceless woman. "Mister"—you have the title of a gentleman, although you are behaving like a cad. "Mister"—you see, I treat you with all possible politeness, although you have not deserved any such respect from me. There is irony in the word "Mister"; it makes one long for a title.

"Mr. Reeves, I am sorry to say that you are not telling me the truth."

Reeves sat stunned. It was too bad, that he should have thrown away disguises only to be called a liar. It was too bad that Gordon should have been right when he said "Nothing deceives like the truth." He sat there humbled, waiting for more.

"Of course, I don't see at all why you and your friends see fit to treat me in this way. The only thing that seems quite clear to me is that it is unfair to expect me to be frank with you when you are not being frank with me. I am sorry to say that I cannot help you."

"May I say something? I am afraid you feel that you are being left in the dark because I am not telling you everything, all the suspicions we have formed as well as the facts which have come to our notice. I can quite understand that, if that is what you mean, but——"

"I mean nothing of the kind. I mean that the statements which you have made to me are, to my certain knowledge, untrue."

Reeves gave a rather ghastly smile. "Would you mind telling me exactly which statement of mine it is that you call in question?"

"Really, Mr. Reeves, you seem to expect a great deal of me. You come to me, a complete stranger, asking for private information. You ask for it on the ground that you are conducting a private investigation, and you tell me your story. I do not know whether there is a word of truth in your story. I only know that one detail in it is demonstrably false. You now expect me to tell you which that detail is, so that you can correct the only part of your story which I know to be false; is that reasonable? Come now, Mr. Reeves, tell me the whole story again, exactly as it happened, and I will see if I can help you."

"I'm really very sorry, but I have already told you the

truth to the best of my ability. I am afraid I could not alter my 'story,' as you call it, without falsification."

"Well, I am afraid we seem to be at cross purposes. Perhaps it would be best if you conducted your researches independently, since we cannot agree?"

There was no mistaking the hint of the front door about this last suggestion. Reeves rose with what dignity he could muster, and took his leave. It must be regretfully admitted that Gordon received the account he gave of his experiences with tempestuous laughter; and Reeves was glad of that mantle of inaudibility which cuts off the motorcyclist from his side-car when it is in motion.

Carmichael, who met them at the door of the club, was more sympathetic. In his view, Miss Rendall-Smith had given the photograph to Davenant, not realizing his identity with Brotherhood, and had thought it impossible that Davenant should have allowed so precious a document to pass out of his possession. But he was in high spirits, having made, he said, a little discovery of his own.

"You know you told me about your efforts to identify the book from which the cipher was taken—the cipher on the postcard? Well, you went the right way to work, but not, if you will excuse my saying so, taking all the possibilities into account. Supposing that Brotherhood had the actual book with him in the carriage when he left London, you have to remember that he changed at Paston Oatvile. Now, I asked myself, what if, from some carelessness or want of interest, he should have left the book in that first-class railway carriage? That train, you see, stops for good at Paston Oatvile, and is cleaned out there the same night."

"Of course. I was a fool not to think of that."

"Well, I went off to the station while you were away, and repeated your own trick."

"Selecting an imaginary book of your own, I suppose?"

"No; it is always better to put one story about the country-side rather than two. I said that a friend of mine had lost a copy of *The Sorrows of Satan*, and was anxious to recover it. The porter referred me to another porter, THE other porter, to be accurate, and he informed me that he had found, in that train, a copy of a book called *Immortality*."

"But there isn't a book called that."

"I know. Many might be, but none are. However, I saw what was up. The porter, by a train of thought which I find myself unable to follow, had taken the book home to his wife: and it was no surprise to me when she produced a copy of Momerie's *Immortality*. It had been a disappointment to her, it seemed, and she made no difficulty about parting with it."

"But have you any reason for thinking it's the book we're looking for?"

"Yes. There are a lot of lines down the side, queries and shriek-marks occasionally, which convince me that the thing was in Brotherhood's hands. Only, of course, we want your copy of the cipher to read it from."

"Excellent man. Let's come up at once. I ought to be able to lay my hands on it, though I can never be certain. I play a perpetual game with the maid who does my rooms; she always seems to think that documents are more easy to deal with if they're piled up in a great heap, instead of lying scattered about. Every morning I disarrange them, and the next morning, as sure as fate, they are piled up again." They had reached Reeves' room by now. "Let's see; that's the Income Tax, and that's my aunt, and that's that man . . . Ha! what's this? No . . . No . . . this can't be it . . . well, I'm dashed! The thing seems to have gone."

"You're sure you didn't keep it in your pocket?"

"I don't think so . . . No, it's not there. Look here, I'll go through them again . . . You know, it's a very rum thing, because I took another look at that cipher only last night."

"And now it's gone. Anything else missing?"

"Not that I can see. Oh, I say, this is the limit! First of all I got the cipher without the key, and then I get the key without the cipher."

"How like life," suggested Gordon.

"What's this? 'Hold it and thoughts with the . . .' oh, splendid! Look here, I worked the cipher out all wrong in this beastly Formation of Character book. But when I did that, I turned down all the pages I wanted, and underlined the significant words. So old Watson will come in useful after all. Hang on one moment—yes, here it is. Now, ready? The word 'hold' is the fifth word on the seventh line of page 8. What's that in Momerie?"

"That's 'you.' It sounds all right for the beginning of a message."

And so they worked it out, this time more fruitfully. When the process was complete, Carmichael had a half-sheet in front of him on which the words appeared, "You will perish if you go back upon your faith."

"Yes," said Gordon meditatively. "That's too good to be mere coincidence. That was the message—was it a threat or a warning?—which was sent to Brotherhood, and old Brotherhood worked it out, presumably, in his Momerie, but wasn't in time to profit by it. The only thing is, now we've got it, it doesn't seem to get us much further."

"It means, I suppose," said Carmichael, "that Brotherhood had promised to do something, and was trying to back out of it."

"Possibly that," said Reeves.

"Why possibly? What else could it mean?"

"Oh, I don't know . . . No, of course; that's it. But, as Gordon says, it doesn't seem to get us much further."

"Not in itself," agreed Carmichael. "But meanwhile it has incidentally provided us with an extra clue."

"What's that?" asked Gordon.

"I'll tell you some other time. I say, it's time for luncheon. Let's go down."

And it was not till they were downstairs that he explained his meaning. "The other clue is the disappearance of the cipher. There's more in that than meets the eye, unless I'm mistaken."

CHAPTER XI

A FUNERAL AND A VIGIL

"I DON'T quite see what you mean," said Reeves as they sat down to luncheon.

"Never mind," said Carmichael, "we shall see if I'm right or not. Meanwhile, there's the funeral this afternoon, and it would hardly be decent to take any action till after that, would it? Hullo, Marryatt, what time does the thing start?"

"Half-past two. A good many of the members mean to turn out, and one wanted them to get away in time for an afternoon round. I must say, I think the club's done handsomely by poor Brotherhood, considering how few of us really knew him. The Committee has sent a very fine wreath."

"And that's the only one, I should think," said Gordon.

"Oddly enough, it isn't. There's one other, a peculiarly expensive-looking thing, which came down from London. There's no name on it, no inscription of any kind, in fact."

"H'm!" said Reeves; "that's curious."

"My dear Reeves," expostulated Gordon, "I'm not going to have you examining the wreaths on the coffin with your lens and forceps. There are limits of decency."

"Well, I won't worry about it anyhow till Carmichael has—Hullo! hit him on the back, Gordon." For Carmichael had been overtaken by one of those choking fits which the best-behaved of us are liable to.

"It's a curious thing," he gasped on recovering, "that one always used to say, when one was small, that one's drink had 'gone the wrong way.' Nothing at all to do with the wind-pipe, I believe."

The funeral was, it must be confessed, a riot of irony. The members who attended had decided that it would look bad to take their clubs with them to the churchyard, but their costumes were plainly a compromise between respect for the dead and a determination to get on with business as soon as it was over. None of them had any tears to shed. The village of Paston Oatvile turned out to a child in sheer morbidity, to see " 'im as fell down off of the railway put away." The sonorous assurances of the burial service had to be read out in full earshot of the village green on which, little more than a week ago, Brotherhood had laboriously disproved the doctrine of personal immortality. To these same solemn cadences the great lords of Oatvile, ever since they abandoned the Old Faith under William III, had been laid to rest within these same walls—

> Some with lives that came to nothing, some with
> deeds as well undone

—and yet there had been a sort of feudal dignity about

their manner of departing. But this unknown sojourner of a day, who had known hardly a soul in the parish, who had loved nothing of all that country-side except eighteen little holes in the ground, what mourning could there be for him—the body so mangled, the soul whose existence he had denied?

One understood why people wanted to be cremated. While we keep all our seriousness for our frivolities, what wonder that men feel a sense of disproportion about the traditional solemnities of interment? With the villagers, indeed, it was different—you might almost say that the hour of their funerals was the hour they lived for. It made them one with the earth they had tilled and furrowed; it gave them, at last, a permanent tenure among their own immemorial fields. "Man that is born of woman is full of sorrow and hath but a short time"—they had learned, unconsciously, to measure their lives by the secular oaks in the great park, by the weather-beaten antiquity of the village church itself. But this strange race of light-hearted invaders, to whom each spot of ground was no more than a good lie or a bad one, what part had they in the communal life of these retired valleys? It meant nothing to them.

We have been following the service with Gordon's eyes; Reeves, it is probable, was lost in speculation as to the donor of the mysterious wreath, and Carmichael was doubtless reminded of a thousand things. But it was over at last, and Reeves, eager to get back to business, im-

plored Carmichael to explain his hints about the
disappearance of the cipher. "Wait till we get back to
your room," was the only answer. And, when the desired
haven was reached, "Have another look among those
papers, and make certain you didn't pass it over by
mistake."

"Good Lord," said Reeves suddenly, "here it is! But I
swear it wasn't when I looked before. I say, Carmichael,
have you been playing the funny ass with the thing?"

"No," said Carmichael, "I haven't."

"Who has, then?"

"That's the point. I should be glad if I were in a
position to enlighten you. You see, I know the maid was
blameless as regards that piece of paper. She only does
the rooms early in the morning; now, I came in after
breakfast, when you'd gone off to Binver, to have another
look at the cipher and see if I could make anything of it
by inspection. And it was still there."

"And you're sure you didn't take it away with you?"

"Positive. Now, observe this: that document must have
been taken away while you and Gordon were both at
Binver, while I was over at the station."

"But how did it get back there?"

"It was put back there. And it was put back there, not
during luncheon, for I had another look afterwards, but
while we were down at the funeral. It follows that none
of our party this afternoon has been meddling with your

papers—I'm glad to think, for example, that the Secretary escapes suspicion."

"But do you seriously mean to say there's somebody in this house who comes into my room and disturbs my papers for his own ends?"

"Don't be so shocked about it. You've been spending the last three days spying on other people; is it impossible that other people should spy on you? Look here, that paper is in your room at half-past ten; it is no longer there at half-past twelve; it, is back again at four o'clock. Do you mean to tell me that somebody acquainted with your habits hasn't been meddling with your papers?"

"What made you suspect it?"

"That's the odd thing. Did you ever notice how often a false calculation puts you on the track of a true one? Puzzling over that odd experience we had last night about the photograph, I found myself wondering whether conceivably some one could have come in and altered it while you were out. Well, upon reflection, that was impossible, because we were in the room the whole time, all four of us. But meanwhile, it did occur to me that perhaps our proceedings were being rather too public. Look how full of comparative strangers this dormy-house is; any one of those may be Brotherhood's murderer, for all we know, or at least an accomplice. And then, when you found the cipher, gone, it occurred to me at once, 'I was right; there is somebody on the spot who is following our movements!' That was why I had that choking-fit at luncheon—you were just going to talk about the disappearance of the cipher in a crowded dining-room; and it seemed to me imprudent."

"But, look here, what's the man's game? Why take the thing away and then put it back again?"

"My dear Reeves, you shouldn't go to funerals, it has a depressing effect on your intelligence. The cipher was taken away this morning, when it might have been of some use to you, I suspect, by somebody who had seen me looking at it and so realised that it was important. Then, by a mere accident, it proved that you did not need the paper after all, and had read the message without it. I saw what would happen—if we left your room empty, the cipher, now useless, would be put back. And that is exactly what happened. The hypothesis has become a certainty."

"Good Lord," said Reeves, walking up and down the room. "What on earth are we to do about it?"

"Keep quiet about our movements for one thing. I shouldn't even discuss them with Marryatt more than you can help: he's a little slow-witted, you see, and a little fond of talking, so anything you say to him may get round. Gordon is different—he's all right. The next point is clear. We must set a trap of some kind, and catch our man red-handed."

"You mean the murderer?"

"Not necessarily the murderer. The man who is

watching us; it may not be the murderer at all."

"But how do you propose to catch him?"

"I propose that two of us—preferably you and Gordon, because I am fond of my sleep—should sit up to-night and watch outside the door. Meantime, we have to excite the curiosity of your visitor so powerfully that he will want to come out and investigate your room. I propose that we should put up a notice (with the Secretary's leave, of course) saying that you have one or two of Brotherhood's books and things which you are prepared to give away as souvenirs to anybody who cared for him; please apply to your rooms to-morrow. And now let's go down and have some tea."

"But I haven't got any of Brotherhood's things," objected Reeves as they went downstairs.

"Exactly. And nobody cared a brass farthing for Brotherhood. But meanwhile, there is every chance that this anonymous gentleman will be interested to see what you have got, and will pay a nocturnal visit to your room. If you see anybody pass, you can fall on him and throttle him. If nobody passes, at about one o'clock I should go to bed if I were you. It's a pity to forgo one's sleep."

"Well, we'd better do the thing thoroughly. I'll go out this evening and come in with a bag, so as to look as if I'd been over and got some things from Brotherhood's house."

"That's a good idea. One moment, I must go over to young van Beuren and get some chewing-gum."

"Carmichael," said Reeves when he got back, "you've been surprising us a good deal lately, but one thing I should never have guessed about you—I should never have imagined that you chewed."

"I don't," said Carmichael, and would answer no more questions on the subject. Nor had Reeves any opportunity to press the point, for Marryatt came in soon afterwards, and sat down at their table. "Is it true?" asked Carmichael, "that Brotherhood is the first member of the club to be buried here?"

"He is. There was Parry, of course, who died here, but he was buried in London. It must be strange for these Oatviles, who have had all the expensive funerals to themselves for the last two hundred years, to make room for an old fellow like that."

"Two hundred? Why not three hundred?" asked Reeves.

"Well, the Oatviles were Catholics, you know, up to James II's time. People say that the room we use as the billiard-room now used to be the chapel at one time. And the Oatviles don't seem to have been buried here till the time of Queen Anne."

"Really, Marryatt?" said Carmichael. "That is most interesting. They must have died abroad, I fancy, for of course Protestant burial was the only kind legal in England. Did it ever occur to you how little early Renaissance architecture you find in English villages? It's an odd testimony, I think, to the vitality of

Catholicism. Puritanism must have had something to do with it, of course, but considering what an itch for architecture the Renaissance brought with it, you would expect more traces of it, if the Laudian religion had ever really taken hold."

"I think, to judge by the parish register, the Oatviles must have been very staunch recusants, and a great trouble to my predecessors. They were important people, too, in the neighbourhood, even before the great house was built, while they lived here at the Dower-house."

Gordon was not acquainted with the evening's programme till after dinner; he accepted his part in it with a wry face; but with pleasurable tremors of excitement. It would be the first time, he said, his revolver would have been loaded since he shot off his last cartridges in November, 1918. There was a small, unoccupied room whose door faced that of Reeves; this door habitually stood ajar, and there was not much likelihood that any unauthorized wanderer would trespass there. Gordon and Reeves were to make their way there quietly at twelve o'clock, and sit there in the dark till one. They pleaded hard to be allowed to play bezique with an electric torch, but Carmichael was firm. Even whispering was not to be carried on except in case of necessity, and to crown their privations, they were warned not to smoke. Until twelve they sat playing bridge in Reeves' room with Marryatt: then the Company dispersed, although Carmichael insisted on being left

behind for a little, while Reeves and Gordon went off
and pretended to undress, "to make sure," he said, "that
our visitor doesn't arrive too early."

It is extraordinary what a lot you can hear, even in a
country house, when you sit for an hour in the dark on
the alert. Expresses whistled through Paston Oatvile; and
one goods train only passed its signals after several
stoppages, each of which meant a repetition of the
musical clink-clink-clink which goods trucks make as
they hit one another. A dog somewhere at the back had a
fit of loneliness, and howled; cats told their nightly tale
of love and hate. Coals fell out of distant grates; the
woodwork creaked uncannily at intervals. But at no
moment was there a step in the passage: nor was any
hand laid on the door of the room opposite. They both
felt cramped and overwatched when one o'clock sounded
from the belfry of the old stables, and they were free to
creep back to their beds.

"I say," whispered Reeves, "why not come into my
room and have a whisky-and-soda before we turn in?"

"Oh," replied Gordon, "didn't Carmichael tell you?
We are not to go into your sitting-room on any account."

"The old brute!" said Mordaunt Reeves. "But I
suppose he knows what he's doing."

CHAPTER XII

A SEARCH WITH PIANO ACCOMPANIMENT

IF Carmichael let his colleagues in for a late sitting, at least he made amends for it himself by unwontedly early rising. Reeves found him fully dressed when, pyjamaed himself, he set out for his morning bath.

"What on earth are you doing," he asked, "wandering about at this hour?"

"Well, you see," said Carmichael, "I had to go and clear up your room before the housemaid came in. Housemaids don't like chewing-gum on their boots." And with this partial explanation Reeves had to be satisfied till they sat down to smoke a pipe after breakfast in a secluded corner of the lounge.

"For Heaven's sake let's have an explanation, "he urged. "There's a chewing-gum *motif* running through life at present which is worrying me more than I can say."

"I don't mind about that," said Gordon; "what worries me is Carmichael being up and dressed at half-past seven."

"Well, if you prefer it, let us put it this way," said Carmichael. "I had to get up early, Reeves, to unlock your room; otherwise the maid wouldn't have been able to tidy it for you."

"To unlock it? When did you lock it, then?"

"When I left it, to be sure, at twelve o'clock last night."

"What! Do you mean to say that Gordon and I sat there for a solid hour waiting for somebody to go into my room, when the door was locked all the time? Look here, Carmichael, if you've simply been pulling our legs——"

"No, I have not been pulling your legs, if I apprehend rightly the meaning of that rather puzzling metaphor. You were waiting for somebody to *try* to get into your room; if he had tried, he would have found two muscular young men tackling him from behind, and the possibility of getting through the door would have had a merely academic interest."

"But I thought you said we were to catch him red-handed? Pretty good fools we should have looked if we had found that it was some guest who'd mistaken his room, or somebody who was wanting to borrow a pipe-cleaner!"

"I admit it. But then, you see, I had an intuition, almost amounting to a certainty, that the visitor who intruded upon your room does not come in through the door."

"Oh, he doesn't? Then you mean that Gordon and I were merely sacrificed to your peculiar sense of humour—we weren't really doing any good? My word, Carmichael——"

"You are always too hasty in leaping to conclusions. You were doing a great deal of good by sitting up in the room opposite. You were convincing the mysterious gentleman that I expected him to come through the door. And it was that conviction which emboldened him to pay you a visit last night. I am sorry to have practised any deception on you two, but really it was the only means that occurred to me for inducing the gentleman behind the scenes to act as he did. And after all, I only made you sit up for an hour."

"An hour," said Gordon, "cannot be properly measured by the movements of a clock, an inanimate thing which registers time but doesn't *feel* it. Many things lengthen time; but three things above ally darkness, silence, and not smoking. The watch we kept last night was a fair equivalent for three hours over a fire with a pipe."

"Well, I apologize. But you will be glad to hear that the experiment succeeded. Somebody did come into your room last night, Reeves, and wandered all over it, though of course he found nothing that was of the slightest interest to him, because there was nothing to find."

"And how do you know all this?"

"That is where the chewing-gum comes in. Secotine would have done: but chewing-gum is more certain. I do not profess to understand why people chew; my impression is that it is merely a kind of fidgeting. Those people who talk about the unconscious would probably tell you that all fidgeting is a form of 'compensation.' Observe that word, for it is the great hole in their logic. Their idea is that So-and-so does not murder his grandmother, but he does twiddle his thumbs. They will tell you, consequently, that twiddling your thumbs is a kind of compensation for not murdering your grandmother. But the whole strength of their case should rest on their ability to *prove* a connexion between the two things, and instead of proving it you will find that they steadily assume it. However, as I was saying —the peculiarity of van Beuren's special chewing-gum is this: that it can be drawn out to an almost indefinite length, and forms a thread of almost invisible fineness. If you stretch such threads, say, between one chair and another all over a room, as I did round your room, Reeves, last night, the great probability is that a casual visitor will walk into it and carry whole strands of it away with him, without noticing anything peculiar."

"What!" said Reeves, "you mean like Sherlock Holmes and the cigarette-ash on the carpet?"

"It was not one of Holmes' more original performances. He had been anticipated, in point of fact, by the prophet Daniel. You should read the story of Bel and the Dragon, Reeves."

"And now," said Gordon, "I suppose we proceed to the station, and take a good look at the trouser-ends of all our club-fellows as they wait for the London train?"

"Why, no. I do not think that method would be very

fruitful. My idea was not to discover *who* it is that visits Reeves' room, but to make sure that there is somebody who does so, and that he does not come through the door."

"In fact, that he comes through the window?"

"No, my dear Gordon, it is not everybody who has your agility in negotiating windows. The windows in question are a good twenty feet from the ground; there is no drain-pipe near them; and anyone who attempted to put a ladder up to them would leave traces among the begonias beneath which even a caddy would not find it difficult to follow up."

"Well, come on, don't be so mysterious. What is it? A secret passage?"

"That seems to be the only sensible solution. One does not, of course, expect a secret passage in a club-house. But then, you see, this is not like other club-houses, and you, Reeves, must have been struck like myself by the significance of what Marryatt was saying last night."

"What was Marryatt saying last night?"

"Why, that the Oatviles were Catholics nay, were noted Recusants, right up to the time of the third William. That means, of course, that they harboured priests; and you could not harbour priests within this distance of London without having a priests' hiding-hole. There was a man, his name escapes me at the moment, who made it his special business to go about constructing these hiding-holes. A priori, then, it is fairly certain that there must be some architectural secret about the old manor-house of the Oatviles. And perhaps in this case they ran to a secret passage."

"Reeves, my boy," said Gordon, "you'll have to keep this dark, or they'll be putting up the rent of your rooms."

Reeves still seemed a little dissatisfied. "But surely, Carmichael, while we were about it we could have kept watch in the room itself, and seen where the hiding-place is, and who comes out of it."

"We could have tried. But tell me: how much of our conversation does this gentleman overhear? And whereabouts in your room could you have hidden with any safety? Honestly, I don't believe he would have come out except while he knew that you and Gordon were busy watching the wrong side of the door."

"You're assuming, of course, that he can't have got in at the door by a duplicate key after Reeves and I went to bed?"

"I am not assuming that, I know it. I took the liberty of putting a bit of that useful chewing-gum across the lock of the door, and it was still undisturbed in the morning. Whereas the chewing-gum which stretched between the chairs had been ploughed up in every direction."

"As it is, though, we've still got to find the entrance to the passage."

"As you say. I thought we might spend a happy morning looking for it. Let's see, there is a piano in your rooms; do you play it?"

"Very badly."

"That's exactly what we want."

"How do you mean?"

"Why, if you sit in your rooms playing the piano, the gentleman on the other side of the partition will probably assume that nothing much is happening. If you play it loudly, you will drown any little thumping noises we may happen to make. And if you play it very badly, the gentleman on the other side, if he is at all musical, will probably retreat to the utmost limits of his hiding-place."

"But look here," said Gordon, "we're not certain this man is the murderer. Is it quite humane——"

"Oh, shut up," said Mordaunt Reeves. "You're right, Carmichael, as usual. What's wrong with starting now?"

Reeves, it must be confessed, did his part of the programme admirably. He even sang to his own accompaniment. When he got to "Land of Hope and Glory," Gordon asked if he might not have cotton-wool in his ears. He also expressed a fear that all the other residents would come in asking Reeves to stop. But fortunately it was a time of day at which the residents are either in London on business, or going round the links like sensible men.

Meanwhile, under cover of Reeves' barrage, the search was proceeding busily. "The ceiling," said Carmichael, "is out of the question. Even if there was concealed trap-door in it, it would be too risky to let down ladders and pull them up again. Now, about the floor? There's this felt undercarpet—I suppose that's nailed down all right, Reeves?"

> "Wider sti-ill, and wider," sang Reeves,
>   "Nailed it down myself;
> Bought it Tottenham Court Road
>   Just a yea-ear ago."

"Well, nobody's been in a position to take liberties with the carpet, that's clear, and it goes right up to the edges of the floor, so I think we may rule the floor out too. Now, Gordon, you've four walls to choose from— one with the door in it, one opposite with the windows in it, one with the fireplace in it, and one blank, where the book-case stands. Which are you betting on?"

"I'm not betting on any. But I'm maintaining that the door wall is the one to search first, because we've only to open the door to see what thickness it is."

"There's something in that. Hullo! The door does stand in a bit of a recess. Where's that tape measure? A foot and a half—hardly good enough, is it? You see, if you tap the panelling here the sound is quite dull, and that means there's brick behind the panelling. And there's something thicker than mere plaster on the passage side too. The mysterious gentleman can't be quite as thin as all that. No bulges in the wall, except of course that big oak chest. Do you know what's inside that chest, Reeves?"

"Yes, I ken that chest, it's as full as can be
With my own odds and ends, and it's all full of drawers,
And the key's on the mantelpiece if you don't believe me
    With his hounds and his horn in the morning,"

was the reassuring, if not very metrical, reply.

"Then that does for the wall. Now, the window wall's thick; you can see that from the window recesses. On the other hand, it's got to carry the thickness of the outer wall, and the outer walls of Tudor buildings are generally pretty thick. Artillery, you see, had abolished the castle idea, but from force of habit they went on making their outside walls thick, because you never knew what might happen. And of course some of these brick houses did stand siege—you know Aston Hall, I expect, in Birmingham. It sounds genuine when you tap it, doesn't it?"

"Yes," said Gordon, listening. "Besides, if you come to think of it, this house is pre-Reformation. There was no reason why they should want a secret passage in it when it was built. But when the bad times started, and they wanted a refuge for the priests, the man who came to build the hiding-place wouldn't play any tricks with a great solid outside wall. He would surely run up a false partition between two rooms."

"Admirable," said Carmichael. "It looks as if we should have to trespass on Reeves' neighbours. Reeves, who lives in the rooms next yours?"

"The one on the left," SANG REEVES, "is Colonel Steele;
    I fancy you both must know him,
And Mr. Murdoch's on the right,
    He plays the 'cello, blow him!
Both of them work in London Town,
    So they're both of them out this morning;
Of that there is no matter of doubt,
No possible, probable shadow of doubt,
    No manner of doubt whatever."

"Good," said Gordon. "I'll step the rooms, shall I, while you step the passage? We hardly need the tape-measure yet."

"Better do both, if you won't mind; then the pace will be the same." And Carmichael busied himself in wandering round the room looking for cracks till Gordon reappeared. "Well," he said, "what news?"

"The fireplace wall, I fancy," said Gordon. "From the door of Colonel Steele's room to the door of this, walking down the passage, it takes twelve strides. Inside his room, I only take five strides to the wall. Inside this room, I take a bit over five strides to the same wall. Therefore there must be a thickness of about a pace and a half between Colonel Steele's room and Reeves'. Now one comes to think of it, he wouldn't hear Murdock's 'cello if there was that thickness the other side."

"A pace and a half? The priests must have been on the thin side. Yes, that would be it: there must be a length of about ten feet from the fireplace to the wall on the side of the fireplace opposite to the window. Somewhere in that ten feet we've got to find the spring."

"Good heavens!" said Gordon suddenly, "suppose there's a sliding panel."

"A man couldn't get through one of these panels — not even you, Gordon, in your well-known human-cobra act," said Reeves, who had stopped singing for the moment.

"No, but a man might put his arm through it, and take the photograph away, and put another in its place, while the people in the room were closely occupied—arranging their hands at bridge, for example."

"You've got it!" said Carmichael. "But why, why?" He and Gordon both went to the spot where the photograph had rested on the cornice two nights before. There was a crack near it, through which it might be possible for a man standing in the dark beyond to keep a watch on the inside of the room, but this crack seemed to hold no further secret. It was Gordon who eventually, fingering the little mouldings on the lower side of the cornice, found one which pushed upwards, acting as a sort of latch. A little tug at the remaining mouldings made the panel turn sideways and disclose a triangular opening of a few inches across, through which Reeve's vociferous rendering of "Annie Laurie" burst into the stillness of the priests' hiding-place.

CHAPTER XIII

THE MAN IN THE PASSAGE

"WELL," said Gordon, "what do we do next?"
"The first thing," said Carmichael, "is to shut up this hole again exactly as it was. The next thing is to discuss what we do next. And, Reeves, I think it might be best if you went on playing for a little."

"If music be the food of detection," agreed Gordon, "play on. Give us excess of it, that surfeiting the mysterious gentleman behind the panelling may sicken, and so die. Well, he can't have come through that hole, can he?"

"No," said Carmichael, "but there's certain to be another catch just inside which will open the secret door. You see, that hole is obviously for a man to put his arm through. And as the arm-hole opens from this side, the catch of the door will clearly open from the other. But, just personally, I don't very much want to open that door without, considering first what we're going to find on the other side. Is the man armed, for example? Is there likely to be another opening he can escape through? I confess to an aversion from taking any risks."

"If he came here straight from the railway," said Reeves from the piano, "he wouldn't be likely to have any firearms with him."

"But you forget," said Gordon, "he must have an accomplice outside; somebody who brings him food— why not weapons too?"

"It's a conceivable plan," said Carmichael, "to keep a look-out and catch this confederate of his. Because the confederate presumably uses some other entrance, and if we found that . . ."

"We could wait at that end, and let Reeves go on playing the piano to him; he couldn't stick it much longer. No, that's all very well, but I really think we ought to do something at once, before this man sees that there's something up, and possibly makes a bolt for it. I know the direct method sounds silly, but I propose that we should go in and take a look round. I don't mind going first."

"I don't see much good in all three of us going in. What happens if our man breaks cover through the other entrance? You see, it may be a member of the club all the time; who could turn up smiling at the other end, and nobody have a right to question him."

"One moment," said Carmichael. "Now we come to think of it, we do know where the other end of the passage was. We know that the old chapel was the present billiard-room. Why not lock this door, and go down to have a look at the billiard-room? You and Gordon can have a game, or pretend to, while I take a look round the walls."

This adjustment was agreed upon, and they found the billiard-room unoccupied. It seemed, however, to show signs of recent habitation, for the dust-cloth had been taken off the table, the balls were out, and a cue laid across one corner as if to indicate that they were not to be disturbed. But this was voted accidental: the red was on spot, and the plain ball spotted in balk; spot was in balk, obviously as the result of a deliberate miss. And a glance at the score-board showed that spot had not scored, while plain had scored one from spot's miss. In fact, it appeared that two people had started a game, and interrupted it after the first stroke, a miss in balk.

"Come on," said Gordon: "nobody can want to have those balls left undisturbed." And the two proceeded to play, with a good deal of noisy conversation, while Carmichael investigated the walls.

"You see," he said, "the same old pattern of cornice in the panelling. With any luck the spring will be the same." And, sure enough, before ten minutes were up he had identified the spring.

"That settles it," said Gordon. "We'll get Marryatt, and he and Carmichael can keep watch outside the billiard-room door. Reeves and I will go down the passage from upstairs, with an electric torch: my experience of fighting in the dark is that the man who has got the electric torch, so that he can see and can't be seen, has got the upper hand from the start."

Marryatt was found without difficulty, and consented to mount guard after a minimum of explanation. Carmichael was provided with a revolver, chiefly *ad terrorem*, for he had no idea how to use it; Marryatt, true to medieval principle, was only armed with a niblick. Gordon took another revolver and an electric torch, and went back again with Reeves to the upper opening. When the panel had been pushed back, it needed but a little fumbling on the inner side to discover a latch. When this was lifted, they found that the wall opposite them yielded to the touch, and a whole section of the panelling turned on a vertical axis, the right side of it coming outwards into the room, the left vanishing into the passage. The work was of miraculous fineness, and when they shut the door again they had difficulty in seeing where the cracks came in the morticing of the old beams.

"Those priests were well hidden," said Gordon. "I imagine the people who hunted them out simply broke down all this stuff with hatchets. But the Secretary could hardly approve of that. Otherwise, I suppose we're very much in the position of the Sheriff's men."

"And the man inside is very much in the position of the priest."

"Except for one circumstance."

"Namely?"

"Guilt," said Gordon.

"Well , what happens next?"

"A little Dutch courage." Gordon helped himself to a liberal glass of neat whisky. "If I were Carmichael, you

would have a little lecture at this point on the origin of
the phrase 'Dutch courage.' Dating, you see, my dear
Reeves, from the seventeenth century, the last time when
we were seriously at war with the Dutch. Meanwhile, I
wish we were still at war with the Germans, and this
were a German dug-out. Because then we should simply
stand at the entrance with a bomb and tell them to come
out. But there again I suppose the Secretary wouldn't be
best pleased—really, he's becoming a nuisance, that
Secretary."

"You still haven't told me how we're going to
proceed."

"We proceed with me in front and you behind. I have
the revolver, you have the electric torch. You hold it at
arm's length, just in front of my shoulder. That ought to
puzzle the other man if it comes to shooting.
Conversation will be conducted in a low tone of voice.
If we find nobody there, we emerge at the billiard-room
end, and tell Carmichael he's a fool."

"Good. I'm not really certain, when all's said and
done, that I really want to meet this man. Curiosity has
its limits, I find."

"Well, are you ready? Flash the light into the passage
as soon as I open the door. Then let me go in first, and
follow up close."

The passage was startlingly high, having the whole
height of the outer room. It was so narrow that you
instinctively edged sideways along it, though there was

just room to walk breast-forward and avoid contact with the cobweb-matted walls.

It began to descend almost immediately, by a series of wooden steps; and by a rough calculation Gordon made out that they were below the level of Reeves' floor by the time they had reached the parallel of Reeves' inner wall. At this point they had to stoop, a circumstance which rather confused their plan of campaign; and it was clear that this part of the hiding-place was subtracted, not from the thickness of the walls but from the depth of the floor. There was a sharp turn to the right, which showed that they were now following the course of the passage which led past Reeves' room. The dust on the floor of the passage was thick and fine, easily showing the traces of confused, but recent, human footprints.

Quite suddenly the passage opened out to the left, and at the same time a very meagre ray of light from outside attracted their attention. They found a chamber some seven feet square, with a tiny squint to let in the light, from some unnoticeable chink in the brickwork of the outer wall. The height of this chamber was still such that a full grown man could not stand up without stooping, but the presence of light and air made it contrast agreeably with the passage outside. Some attempt, too, had been made to sweep the floor, the dust being all brushed up into a pile at one corner. There could be no doubt that this chamber had been the refuge of hunted priests three centuries back; no doubt, either, that it had been the refuge of a hunted man within the last few days past.

Of the former occupation, indeed, there were few signs. A scratch had been made now and again in the plaster of the walls, giving a name in initials—a tourist's trick, but rescued from vulgarity by the circumstances of its origin, and by the addition of a few Christian symbols—a Cross several times, and once the IHS monogram. Just where the light of the little window fell strongest, a few lines of pious doggerel had been scrawled, difficult to read in their crabbed seventeenth-century handwriting. A sconce for a candle, nailed into the wall, was the only solid monument left of these distant memories.

The eye was more immediately challenged by the evidences of a recent visitor's presence. One expected a rude pallet of straw; a simpler resting-place had been contrived with three cushions obviously looted from the club lounge. There was a candle-end stuck in an empty claret-bottle, and two candles in reserve. There were numerous cigarette-ends thrown carelessly on and around the dust-heap at the corner; all these were of a common and undistinctive brand. There was a rather crumpled copy of Friday's *Daily Mail*, probably derived from the same source as the cushions. There was a tin of boot-polish and a brush, as if the stranger had been careful about his appearance even in these singular surroundings. These relics Reeves quickly reviewed with absorbed interest, and then turned to Gordon in despair.

"All these traces," he said, "and not one that you could call a clue. If the man has escaped us, he has escaped us without leaving a solitary hint of his identity."

"That hardly surprises me," said Gordon. "Of course the man has been in a sense your guest, but you could hardly expect him to sit down and write you a Collins."

"One might have expected one crow of triumph."

"Perhaps that was one in the billiard-room."

"In the billiard-room?"

"Yes, somebody had left you a miss in balk"

"Do you really think . . ."

"Oh, I don't know. Let's go on exploring."

All this time, except for their own whispers, there had been no noise in the secret passage. Through the little window sounds came from a distance, rarefied as sounds are when they come through a small opening. A motor-cycle hooted several times: somebody shouted "Fore!" on the links: far below (as it seemed) somebody was filling a bucket. They crept out again into the passage, the torch switched on again: for some twenty paces they were on the level, then they began to descend, and almost immediately the ceiling grew higher above them—they were in a wall-space instead of a floor-space once more. Just as they reached the foot of the steps, an unforeseen development threw all their plans into confusion—the passage branched in two directions, one branch going straight on, the other turning off sharply to the right.

"What do we do here?" whispered Reeves, flashing the torch up either corridor in turn. "Whichever way we go, it seems to me, we may be taken from the rear."

"I know; we must chance it. We can't separate, because we've only got one torch. We'll try the branch that goes straight on, but be ready to turn round at a moment's notice."

This passage, after a short distance, seemed to terminate in a blank wall. But there was a crack in the wall and Gordon, bending down, saw through the crack the billiard-room as they had left it a quarter of an hour ago, the balls still in position, the door still shut behind which Carmichael and Marryatt were on guard.

"Switch the light higher up," he whispered.

Surely Reeves' torch was giving more light than usual? It seemed to have suddenly doubled its brightness. And then, just as he realized that another torch had been turned on from behind them, a strange voice came out of the darkness:

"Now then, you there, I've got you covered. You this side, drop that torch . . . . That's right: now, you in front, put that revolver down . . . . Now turn and go back the way you came."

It was humiliating, but there was nothing to be done. They had been taken in the rear by somebody coming up the other arm of the passage; they could see nothing of him, looking straight into the light of his torch. He stood at the junction of the two branches to let them pass, still invisible: as they went back on their tracks, Gordon had a wild idea of doubling into the priests' room, but he saw it would be hopeless. He would be unarmed, caught in a trap, with a man who was probably already a murderer covering him with a revolver. They went on, an ignominious procession, right up to the opening in Reeves' room, which they had left ajar behind them.

"Step right out, said the voice, and don't stir till I tell you."

Obediently they crept out into Reeves' room, expecting the stranger to shut the door behind them and fasten it in some way still unknown to them. It was a surprise to both of them when the secret entrance was once more blocked with the shadow of a human form, and they were followed into the daylight by a quite unmistakable policeman.

CHAPTER XIV

A CHASE, ENDING WITH A SURPRISE

"NOW then," said the policeman, falling back on a formula in face of an unexpected situation. "What's all this about?"

There can be no doubt that, on most occasions, the sense of humour is a handicap in life. It implies introspection, and he who introspects is commonly lost. But laughter is, in great part, the child of innocence, and it is doubtful if anything could have exculpated the two amateur detectives from the charge of being criminals so speedily as the complete break-down of Gordon's gravity when the question was asked.

"What are you doing in these rooms?" asked the policeman, less suspicious but by no means more friendly.

"Well, you see," said Reeves, "they're my rooms."

"I ought to warn you," the policeman pointed out, "that this may involve you in a serious charge. We have reason to think that a murderer has been hiding in that passage there. Say nothing if you don't want it to be used as evidence." And he took out the inevitable note-book which is the policeman's substitute for a thunderbolt.

"I'm sorry, officer," said Gordon, "but you must see that we've been going round one another in circles. You're looking for a murderer—let me make a rash guess, and put it to you that it's Brotherhood's murderer you're looking for? Well, we're doing exactly the same. It seems that, by a mere chance, he's been taking refuge in a passage which communicates with this room which is rented by Mr. Reeves here. And instead of finding the murderer, we've found one another."

"Very irregular, gentlemen. You know as well as I do that if you've any information in your possession which might lead to the conviction of the criminal, it's your duty to communicate it to police. Of course, I'm very sorry if I gave you gentlemen a fright, but you've got to look at it this way, Whose business is it to see justice done, yours or mine? You see, if it hadn't been for you gentlemen giving the alarm, not meaning to, I'm not saying you meant to, but if you gentlemen hadn't given the alarm, I might have got this chap bottled up properly in the passage there; and now how am I to know where he is? That's the way you've got to look at it."

"But the coroner's jury brought in a verdict of suicide," objected Reeves.

"Ah, that may be; but you see it's this way, the Force isn't tied down by what the coroner's jury says, and if the Force has its suspicions, then it acts accordingly; and if anybody else has their suspicions then it's their duty to communicate them to the police, d'you see? And then the police can act accordingly."

"Well, I'm very sorry if we've interfered with your plans at all," said Gordon, seeing that the Olympian rage was taking its normal course, and simmering down into a flood of explanatory platitude. "We were meaning to take a little something after all that hunting about in the wainscoting; it's dusty work. I suppose it's no good asking you to join us, Inspector?"

"Sergeant, sir, is what I am. Of course, it's against the regulations, strictly speaking, when on duty; but if you was to offer me something just to show there's no offence taken, why then I won't say No to a glass." And, as the pledge of amity began to flow, Jove ratified his compact by the infallible formula, "Here's to your very good health, gentlemen."

Reeves felt that the moment had arrived for cooperating with Scotland Yard. The fact that Scotland Yard, with no golf balls and no photographs to guide it, no Carmichael and no chewing-gum to aid it, had after all got on the track of the right criminal, began to impress him.

"Well, Sergeant," he said, "there's not much sense in either of us playing a lone hand, is there? What I'm asking myself is, why shouldn't you and we hunt in couples?"

"Very sorry, sir; of course, any information you may see fit to give the police will be acted on accordingly; but you see it's against our regulations to take civilians

about with us when we're on duty, that's how it is. Not
but what, as it's all between friends, I don't mind taking
you gentlemen downstairs and showing you the other
door of that there passage as you didn't see and I came
in by."

The fact that Carmichael was still at his useless post
occurred to the two friends at this point, and made them
consent to the indignity of a personally conducted tour.
"In a cellar the other door is, but it's a cellar you have to
get to from the outside," the sergeant explained, leading
the way downstairs. They were not destined to complete,
on that occasion, their experiences of the passage. They
had only just got out of the front door when the whirlwind
figure of a second policeman almost cannoned into them,
and their attention was directed to a motor-cycle, with
side-car, just disappearing through the lodge gates.

"It's 'im," panted the new-comer. "Gone off on the
blinking bus!"

The mystery man had disappeared, and disappeared,
with singular effrontery, on the very vehicle on which
the representatives of the law had come to track him
down.

"Come on, Sergeant," shouted Reeves, rising to the
occasion. "I've got my car only just round here, and she'll
do a better pace than anything else you could pick up!"
And, while the agitated sergeant explained to Gordon
the message he wanted telephoned to the station at
Binver, Reeves did a record time in starting and bringing

round to the front his new Tarquin "Superbus." It was
scarcely three minutes since the disappearance of the
adventurous stranger when the two policemen, one at
Reeves' side and one luxuriously cushioned in the
tonneau, bounded off down the drive in pursuit.

"What does that car of yours do, Sergeant? Forty? I
can knock fifty out of this easily, as long as we don't get
held up anywhere. I say, what happens if some of your
friends want to run me in for furious driving?"

"You'd get off with a caution, sir, and it wouldn't be
in the papers. You're all right, don't you worry, as long
as you don't run into anything." Indeed, at the pace
Reeves was making, it seemed highly desirable that they
should not. The motor-cycle was still out of sight, and it
seemed likely enough that they were on a forlorn quest.
About half a mile from the Club the road split into two,
either branch joining the main London road, but one
going southwards and one going northwards to meet it.
Would the fugitive make for the crowded suburbs, or for
the open country to the north? The question was
fortunately decided for them when they saw a more than
usually self-diffusive herd of sheep blocking up the
northern arm. Nobody in a hurry would have tried to
penetrate that bleating barrage when he saw a clear road
to his right. Whatever his plans had been, it must have
been the London direction he had taken. In a moment
they had dived under the railway close to Paston Oatvile
station, and swept round into the open current of the
London main road.

Saturday was not yet far advanced enough to have released its stream of pleasure-traffic, so late in the year especially. Their right of way was disputed only by occasional lorries and market-carts. Two motor-cycles they overhauled, with a spasm of hope each time, which died down upon a nearer view. The road was for the most part a gentle switchback, rising and falling over the long folds of the countryside, and at the top of each incline their eyes swept the stretch in front of them for a sight of the fugitive. The surface in front of the engine seemed to spring into a cascade and jumped out on you suddenly; the sere hedges became streaks of gold.

They had gone ten miles without sighting their quarry, and the sergeant began to grow anxious. "The expresses stop at Weighford," he said, "and that's only a mile or two on." He turned to his colleague behind. "D'you remember what time the express from the north stops at Weighford? Quarter to twelve? That's bad. You see, sir, if he gets to Weighford before we catch sight of him, he may drive through it or he may turn aside to the station; and if he makes for the station he'll most likely catch the express for London."

"So can we, if we don't get held up at Weighford. A quarter to twelve, did you say? I think we ought to do it. But if we don't sight him first, it's a bad lookout. What's that on ahead?"

"That's not the one, sir. Ah, there's the goods sidings; express isn't signalled yet."

Weighford is a straggling, unpleasant town, which seems to cast a blight on the road as it passes through, and they were mercilessly bumped. More than once, too, they had to slow down; and finally, to crown their disappointment, they saw the gates of a level-crossing shut against them. Then, just as Reeves was slowing down, the gates began to swing open, and the sergeant suddenly crowed with delight. "That's him, sir! Got held up at the level crossing, and now he's only half a minute's start of us."

The remainder of the race was a thing only to be remembered in nightmares—the children that only just got out of the way in time, the dog that didn't; the lorry that wanted to turn in the middle of the road. . . . But they had their man marked now, and could see that he was making for the railway; could hear, too, the whistle of the express and the grinding of the brakes as it slowed down into the station. At the further platform a quiet, rural train with the label BINVER was sitting on its haunches and panting after the exhaustion of its last five-mile crawl. The station-master was fortunately found, and the progress of the express held up in the interests of a police search. The fugitive had left the side-car standing at the entrance and lost himself among the passengers before his pursuers could alight.

The search, laboriously and muddle-headedly carried on with the aid of the station officials, lasted some five minutes without any result. Fussy passengers might have been paid by the criminal to delay operations, so ready were they with helpful advice. At last an inspector pointed to a door on the non-platform side of an empty first-class carriage, which was unfastened.

"Got through on to the six-foot way, that's what he's done, and slinking round on the other platform maybe."

"Wrong!" shouted Reeves in a flash of inspiration; "he got through into the Binver train just as it went off, and hadn't time to shut the door properly. Sergeant, it's us for the road again!" The sergeant hesitated, then allowed himself to be fascinated by the theory. The station staff was left with orders to go on searching; the side-car was entrusted to the Weighford police, and, within a quarter of an hour of their arrival, Reeves and the two Binver policemen were tearing back along the main road as fast as they had come down it.

Local trains waste most of their time waiting at stations and chatting to the signalman. When they are on the move, they are not really easy to catch even with a fast motor, especially when they have nearly ten minutes' start. There was no stop, so far as this train was concerned, between Weighford and Paston Oatvile. Paston Oatvile had, of course, been warned to hold up the train on arrival, but the staff there was neither numerous nor intelligent, and it seemed very probable that the elusive passenger would be on his travels again, if they could not be on the platform to intercept him. This time Reeves excelled himself and so did the Tarquin.

There was no doubt about the objective; no mental undercurrent of hesitancy to breed infirmity of purpose. The driver himself became part of the machine, a mere lever in the relentless engine of human justice. Almost all the way the line was visible from the road; and as reach after reach of it was disclosed, three pairs of eyes searched for the puff of smoke that would mark the Binver train.

They saw it at last when they were a full mile off. A moment more, and they were at the station gates almost before the wheels of the train had stopped. Three harassed officials were explaining to irritated passengers that they must keep their seats, please. And so began the cruel, inevitable search for the traveller without a ticket. They found him at last, sitting apparently unconcerned in a first-class carriage; the police did not bring him out, but climbed in after him. Reeves went up to endure the effusive gratitude of the sergeant, and caught sight, as he did so, of the prisoner's face.

It was Davenant.

CHAPTER XV

GORDON TAKES THE OPPORTUNITY TO PHILOSOPHIZE

"IT seems," said Carmichael, blinking through his spectacles, "that I have been mistaken. My old tutor always used to say to me—that was Benger: I suppose he'd be before your time, Gordon? Of course he was—Benger always used to say to me, 'Mr. Carmichael, always follow your nose. You've got a straight nose, Mr. Carmichael, but a crooked brain.' Very witty old chap he was, Benger, always saying things like that."

"It was a dashed funny mistake, too," mused Reeves. "Do you realize that, quite possibly, Davenant may have stood behind that hole in the wall and heard us coming solemnly to the conclusion that he didn't exist? That he never had existed, except as a sort of spiritual projection of old Brotherhood, and now, consequently, he had ceased to exist?"

"And what is still more singular," said Carmichael, "is that so far from helping the cause of justice, we seem to have actually hindered it. For I take it there can be little doubt that it was our tapping and measuring upstairs which put Davenant on his guard and made him bolt."

"Tapping? Measuring?" protested Gordon. "Don't you believe it; it was Reeves singing. I always said the man would beat it if we let Reeves go on like that. I'd have done the same myself."

"I'm not at all sure," said Reeves, "that he may not have found the chewing-gum on his trousers, and formed his own conclusions that way. However, there isn't very much harm done. The police have got their man, with no great inconvenience to anybody except that poor old collie at Weighford. Rather a fine dog it was, and the owner wasn't a bit nice about it when I saw him."

"I suppose," Carmichael asked, "that the police can actually prove Davenant was the murderer?"

"Not a bit of it," said Reeves confidently, "unless they've got more up their sleeve than I think they have."

"But surely," urged Gordon, "if he went to all the trouble of hiding himself like a rat in the wainscoting——"

"That's all very well, but they haven't even proved Davenant was the man in the passage. You see, Davenant was travelling on that train, but it's the train he always does come up by every Saturday. He might say that he hadn't had time to get his ticket; that he had come all the way from London; that the real murderer must have slipped out on to the six-foot way and lost himself on the opposite platform. I don't know that he will say that; of course, he is reserving his defence. But even if they can bring people to prove—people who saw him boarding the train at Weighford—that he was the man we were pursuing, it still doesn't follow that he was the murderer. It's extraordinary, the shifts men have resorted to before now when they thought they were going to be accused of murder, although they were as innocent as you or me. Put it this way—suppose Davenant had actually come up by that train on Tuesday, for reasons best known to himself. He gets to Paston Whitchurch, and then hears of what we found at the third tee. He cannot give any plausible explanation of his coming back here on Tuesday at all. He has some grudge against Brotherhood which we know nothing about. Now, if he can conceal the fact that he came back here at all that day, he escapes suspicion. He knows, somehow, about this secret passage; knows that, as a member of the club, he can wander about here pretty safely without attracting attention. He decides to lie low in the priests' hiding-place till Saturday, and then turn up bright and smiling, knowing nothing about the murder. I say, innocent men have done stranger things before now."

"It sounds pretty thin to me," said Gordon.

"Once more I tell you, it is a fatal habit to proceed from observation to inference, and give inference the name of fact. You say Davenant is the murderer; I say, we don't know that; we only know that Davenant was a man who for some reason expected to be accused of the

murder, and consequently behaved in a very peculiar
way."

"I still don't quite see," said Carmichael, "what
exactly happened while I was waiting outside the
billiard-room door."

"Nothing happened while you were waiting outside
the billiard-room door; it had all happened already. Quite
early on, while we were worrying about up here,
Davenant saw that the place was unhealthy for him. He
wandered out into the billiard-room, arranging the balls,
I think, as a kind of message for us, and then strolled off
somewhere —into the servants' quarters, I suppose. It's
obvious that he must have had a confederate in the house.
Then the police came—I imagine they must have
watched somebody bringing him things from outside."

"Sullivan," said Gordon. "That was what he was
doing, obviously, the day I was over in Davenant's
cottage, he was taking him collars and things."

"Anyhow, the police came and climbed in at the cellar,
making a great song and dance about it as the police
always do. Davenant saw that things were getting pretty
serious, so he made for the nearest motor-bike he could
find—I don't know whether he knew it belonged to the
police or not. Having once started to run away, of course
he couldn't very well stop at Weighford and tell us it
was all a silly mistake: having started to bolt, he had to
go on bolting. And he did it damned cleverly: if he'd

had time to shut the door of the carriage in the express, or had a season ticket to justify his presence in the Binver train, how could he have been caught? That was the train he always came back by on Saturdays."

"I don't think he would have escaped," said Carmichael. "Truth will out—there's a lot in the old saying. By the way, I wonder if either of you know the origin of the phrase *magna est veritas et praevalebit*, or rather *praealet*, to give the exact form?"

"We'll buy it," said Gordon.

Actually it comes from the third book of Esdras. That's a thing ninety-nine people out of a hundred don't know. But what was I saying? Oh, yes, it's extraordinary how criminals don't escape. If you come to think of it, we were close on the track of our man the whole time."

"There," said Gordon, "I can't agree with you. Up to a certain point we were on the right track. Then you came and confused all the tracks with your 'Davenant -is-Brotherhood' slogan. After that we were at a loss— or rather, it was worse than that, we were definitely off the true scent, although the man himself was within a few yards of us. It was only because he came out of his hiding-place and disturbed Reeves' papers—a sheer accident, from our point of view—that we were able to start again. Now, your ideal detective is never dependent upon an accident."

"Well, don't rub it in," suggested Reeves. "After all,

we are both of us as much to blame, because we swallowed Carmichael's theory like lambs."

"Well, as a matter of fact, I never did agree with Carmichael."

"Never did agree with him? Well, you kept jolly dark about it. What weren't you satisfied with about his explanation?"

"Oh, it seemed to me to disregard human probabilities. And, as I told you the other day, I trust human probabilities more than I trust circumstantial evidence. I didn't believe, for example, that the same man could be a Catholic from Saturday to Monday and an atheist for the rest of the week."

"But Carmichael explained that. Surely it's reasonable that a Roman Catholic should want to sweep away what he regards as inadequate theologies?"

"No, it's just what he wouldn't do. I used to know a good many Catholics at one time, and I know a certain amount about their point of view. And they couldn't act in the way Carmichael described, because it would be doing evil in order that good might come of it. And Catholic theology, you see, doesn't allow that."

"I only gave that as a possible explanation," objected Carmichael. "There are plenty of other possible explanations."

"I know. But what's the good of any number of possible explanations when no single explanation is probable? I never can understand the kind of madness that imagines it has solved a difficulty when it has found a whole number of possible explanations that aren't probable. What difference does the number of them make? As a matter of fact, in this case there's only one— that Brotherhood really was an atheist, but posed as a Catholic when he was Davenant merely to put people off the scent. But can't you see how monstrous that is? Instead of taking the trouble to go over to Paston bridge every Sunday, he might have gained a far bigger local reputation for piety by sitting under Marryatt once in three weeks."

"Well, what other human probabilities are there?"

"Next to changing one's religion every Saturday to Monday, the most impossible thing in the world would be to change one's game of golf every Saturday to Monday. Theoretically it sounds all right; in practice I don't believe in it. I can't think how you did either, Carmichael, because golf is a thing of which you *have* some experience."

"Well, why didn't you communicate these doubts to us before?"

"You were talking too hard. But I can produce my diary to show you what I did think about your suggestion." And Gordon disappeared, to return after a few minutes with a formidable volume over which he spent an unvarying twenty minutes every evening. "Here you are. 'Thursday—Carmichael has had an inspiration —he thinks Davenant and Brotherhood were the same person, a sort of Jekyll-and-Hyde pair. He overlooks, it seems to me, the obvious phenomena of religion and golf. But of course it is very typical' " —he broke off. "I don't expect that part would interest you."

"Go on," said Reeves. "I shouldn't have thought Carmichael was typical of anything. What's it all about?"

"Well, the truth is that in this diary I don't merely record what's happened; I've got into the way of philosophizing over it a bit. As you know, Reeves, I've got a bad habit of writing for the papers, and I find writing down my impressions every day often helps me to find subjects."

"It would be a privilege to hear what you made of all this," said Carmichael dryly.

" 'But of course it is very typical,' " Gordon read on, " 'of all these modern philosophies. They are always for explaining something in terms of something else, just as Carmichael wants to explain Davenant in terms of Brotherhood. In plain English it means mixing up two things that are entirely different. The moderns, for example, will have it that punishment is only another name for correction. And once you have said that, the whole idea of punishment drops out of sight altogether. Or they will tell you that a concept is the same as a mental picture, or that Truth is the same as beauty, or as intellectual convenience, or that matter is a form of motion. The root of error is always one of those false identifications, saying that A is B when it isn't.

" 'The cause of them is a rage for the simplification of experience, the result is a paralysis of thought. There is a sense of neatness and efficiency about identifying Davenant with Brotherhood; it explains such a lot—you always can explain a lot by overlooking the facts. But the result is that poor Reeves, who up till now at least had Davenant to hunt for, now regards Davenant as an imaginary being, and is reduced to hunting for an imaginary murderer. Just so it looks very neat and efficient to say that punishment is the same thing as correction; it explains a puzzling idea, simplifies your thought. But what you have done is to banish the whole idea of punishment from your mind, and turn a real thing into a mental figment.

" 'But this theory of Carmichael's makes an even prettier parable of the great and unpardonable error which tries to make one thing out of matter and Spirit—tells you that Spirit is a mode of matter, or the other way round. Just as Carmichael will have it that Davenant is a mode of Brotherhood. Like the materialist or the idealist he is stultifying experience for the sake of a formula. Couldn't one write this up, somehow? Brotherhood, representing Matter, leaves off where Davenant, representing Spirit, begins. Carmichael, representing the modern mind, finds this an excellent reason for supposing that they are really, somehow, the same thing. The materialist sees Brotherhood everywhere, the Idealist sees Davenant everywhere, and consequently neither of them can solve the detective mystery of existence. It looks as if one could work up a sort of Oriental mythology out of it, as good as most Oriental mythologies anyway. And the joke of it is that Davenant's really round the corner the whole time.' I say, that was a pretty good shot anyhow. Why, Carmichael, I even seem to have anticipated your discovery of the secret passage."

"H'm," said Carmichael; "there are some interesting half-truths in all that."

CHAPTER XVI

REEVES PROMISES TO DO HIS BEST

THE conversation recorded in the last chapter took place (I forgot to say) on Saturday afternoon. It was while he was at tea downstairs that a message was brought in to Reeves telling him that a lady wished to see him on urgent business. She would not give her name, but she was waiting for him in what was called "the small lounge"—a dreary little room, which had something of the air of a hospital waiting-room; she would be glad if he could come as soon as possible. Disregarding Gordon's suggestion that he should take Carmichael with him as a chaperon, he made his way to the small lounge with some feeling of self-importance, and found himself most unexpectedly confronted with Miss Rendall-Smith.

"I'm afraid you think badly of me, Mr. Reeves," she said, "and you'll probably think worse of me before I've finished." (Reeves gurgled dissent.) "The other day I turned you out of the house and told you to your face you were a liar. And that's a bad introduction for me when I have to come to you, as I come now, asking for your help."

Reeves was horribly embarrassed. You can offer

whisky to a policeman to show there is no ill-feeling, but it is more difficult to offer it to a lady. "I'm sure I should be very glad to be of any use," he said. "I seem somehow to have made a bad impression on you the other day, though I still haven't the least idea how. Wouldn't it really be better if we put all our cards on the table and treated one another frankly?"

"That's just what I want to do. And, as a sort of guarantee of good faith, I'm going to tell you exactly what it was that made me suspicious of you the other day. You brought me a photograph of myself and told me you had found it on the body of the man who was killed. Now, I was quite prepared to believe you; he had got, and I knew he had got, a photograph of me. But the photograph you showed me was not the one I gave him. It was a portrait taken on the same occasion, at the same sittings but it was in a slightly different pose. So I thought, you see, that you were setting a trap for me. Your manner was so dreadfully Come-now-young-woman-I-know-all-about-you, that I really thought you were a policeman, and were trying to bluff me in some way . . . No, I haven't finished yet. There was one person living round here who *had* a copy of the other photograph, the same kind as you showed me. And that was Mr. Davenant, whom they arrested this morning as the murderer."

"I see. Yes, of course you must have thought I was trying it on. The fact is, I don't yet know exactly how that photograph got into my possession, but I can give a guess now, which I couldn't have then." And he described in outline the discovery of the secret passage and the sliding panel. "You see, if it was Davenant who was behind that panelling all the time, it was quite possible for him to take away the portrait we found on Brotherhood, and to put the portrait you gave him there instead. I can't think why he should have wanted to do it; but there were four of us who all thought at the time that the photograph looked different when we took it down from the cornice. And that's quite natural if it really was a different one."

"Well, all that gets us into the reason why I called. Mr. Reeves, are you working in any sort of co-operation with the police?"

"No. I helped the police by taking them to Weighford and back in my motor, but I'm not working for them, I'm working on my own. To tell the truth, I haven't very much confidence in the intelligence of the police, or in their methods." He omitted, somehow, to mention that the co-operation of civilians was contrary to police regulations.

"In that case I can speak freely. But I want you to understand, please, that I tell you all this in complete confidence so far as the police are concerned. Now, will that be all right? I mean, I suppose you will be called as a witness."

"I suppose that they can only call me as a witness of how I found the body on Tuesday, and how I took the police to Weighford to-day. There is no reason why they should expect me to have any theories about who the murderer was. I think it will be all right."

"Well, I'll risk it, anyhow. You see, I know that the police, once they've caught a man, will always want to convict that man, merely so as to save themselves trouble, and save their own faces."

"That's my experience of them, certainly." Reeves had no experience in the matter whatsoever, but there was no harm in agreeing.

"Well, I'd better tell you about myself first of all, and how I come to be mixed up in the business. My name isn't, legally, Miss Rendall-Smith, although it was my maiden name. My legal name is Mrs. Brotherhood."

"You mean that you are——"

"His widow. It must be a wonderful thing to be a detective, Mr. Reeves."

Reeves was thrilled with the compliment, which a more introspective person might have suspected of irony. He suddenly remembered that a detective ought to have a note-book, and write down facts in it. He had no notebook, so he said, "Excuse me," and fetched a sheet of the club note-paper. On this he wrote down in pencil "Miss R.-S. = Mrs. B." It looked rather silly, somehow, when he had written it.

"I was brought up in these parts, Mr. Reeves. My father used to be Rector of Binver. When that photograph was taken—those photographs were taken, my father was still alive, and I was still unmarried. The only person who'd ever asked me to marry him was Mr. Davenant—I expect you know that he belongs to these parts too."

"I didn't actually know it." The phrase suggested that Reeves might have inferred it, but had not any direct information on the point. "I suppose he didn't live at the Hatcheries then?"

"No, his people had a house near here, which has been pulled down since. His mother, of course, was an Oatvile."

"To be sure." Reeves sucked his pencil, and wrote down "Mr. Davenant senior m. Miss Oatvile." Then a light burst upon him—"Good heavens!" he said, "then that's why he knew about the secret passage?"

"He would, of course. He's told me that he used often to play here when he was a boy. Then there was a coolness between his people and the Oatviles, I think because his people became Catholics. No quarrel, you know, only they didn't see so much of each other after that. Anyhow, Mr. Davenant was badly in love with me and wanted me to marry him. I wouldn't—partly because I wasn't quite sure whether I liked him, partly because my father was very Low Church, and he'd have been certain to make trouble over it. Then the Davenants left the place, and I did too after my father died; and we didn't see any more of one another."

"When was that?"

"Three or four years before the war—1910 I suppose

it must have been. I started out to work for a living, because my father hadn't left us very well off. And then, quite soon, I met this man Brotherhood. He proposed and I accepted him—you mustn't ask me why, Mr. Reeves. That's a thing even detectives can't find out about, why women fall in love with men. I'll only mention that at that time he wasn't a bit rich. After I married we lived in a rather horrid house in Kensington. I never knew anything about his Stock Exchange business much, though I always had an idea that it wasn't very safe, if it was even honest. He began to make money quite soon; and then, you see, he made the whole of it over to me. He was afraid, of course, that he might go bankrupt, and he wanted to have a good reserve which his creditors couldn't touch. I was always rather a fool about business, or I suppose I should have minded the arrangement. As it was, I just thought it very nice of him, and we made arrangements to take a house in the country. I wanted Binver, because it was one of the few places where I'd any friends.

"Then, quite suddenly, I found out about him. I don't mean about his business; I mean about his private life. There are lots of atheists who are very nice people; my husband wasn't one of them. I somehow feel that he chucked over morals first and religion afterwards, if you know what I mean, not the other way about."

Reeves wrote down "Brotherhood not only - God but - morals"; then he scratched it out again. Miss Rendall-Smith went on:

"I didn't want a divorce: you see, I'd been rather strictly brought up about those things. And of course he didn't want one, because of the money. Just when I wanted help and advice, I met Mr. Davenant again; and he was furious when I told him about it all. He set to work to try and find out something about my husband's business, and he did discover something (I don't know what it was) which would have ruined him if it had come out. Then he went to my husband and put a pistol to his head, so to speak—blackmailed him really, I suppose. He made my husband take a solemn oath to let me go my own way and never, without my express consent, publish the fact that he'd married me. Then I came down here and took the house in Binver and thought it was going to be all right.

"Quite soon afterwards my husband rented a bungalow, as you know, and came to live at Paston Whitchurch. I think he wanted to keep a watch over me; I think he also wanted to give me the impression that he was behaving better. But, as he always went away for the week-ends, I didn't feel much interested about that. Once or twice he asked me to come back to him, but of course I wouldn't. When Mr. Davenant came back from the war, he took a house at Paston Whitchurch too, but he could only come there from Saturday to Monday because of his work up in London. I think he just wanted to be near me, and to be able to help me if I was in trouble. And that was the state of things up to last Tuesday. Only my husband had foreseen his bankruptcy, and was making desperate efforts to get me to come back to him. The horrible thing was that I had no hold over him — the secret which would have ruined him once had no terrors for him then—so I'd nothing but his bare word to depend on. And I'm afraid that wasn't much to go upon.

"I knew nothing about what happened on Tuesday till I saw it in the papers. I still don't know how or why the police got the idea that it was Mr. Davenant who murdered my husband. Of course, if they came to know all that I've been telling you now, they'd think it was a certainty. But I've told you about it, because I thought it was best to let you know everything, and then perhaps you could help."

"Of course I should be awfully glad to do anything I could to—well, to establish the innocence of an innocent man. Was that your idea, Miss Rendall-Smith?"

"Mr. Reeves, do you believe at all in a woman's intuitions? Probably you don't, because you go in for clues and all that sort of thing. But I assure you I'm as certain that Mr. Davenant never laid a hand on my husband as I'm certain that you're sitting in that chair. I can't explain the feeling; I can't analyse it; it's like a sort of sixth sense to me. I've always had these strong intuitions, and they've always been right. So I'm asking you, quite fearlessly, to work on this case as hard as you can, and examine all the evidence you've got. I'm perfectly certain that the effect of that will be to prove

Mr. Davenant's innocence. I know he ran away and hid himself; but after all, that's a thing an innocent man may easily do if he's afraid of being charged with murder."

"I was saying the same thing to my friends only this afternoon."

"Mr. Reeves, you're wonderful! And, of course, you've got to remember this. Mr. Davenant is—he's still in love with me. And, you see, he must have known that if he were charged with the murder, my name was likely to get dragged into the thing. So it wasn't only for his own sake that he tried to get away."

"Well, I'll do my best. But you can't throw any light on the whole thing yourself, except for what you've said? You didn't, I mean, see Brother—see your husband or Davenant after you heard about the bankruptcy?"

"Yes, I think I ought to tell you this. Mr. Davenant heard of the bankruptcy—or the strong probability of it—beforehand, and wrote to warn me. So I went up to London to see Mr. Davenant, and came back that same afternoon. He wanted to take me back to Binver on the earlier train, but I wouldn't let him—I didn't want to be seen travelling with him. The result was that he travelled on that fatal train with my husband, and so drew on himself the suspicion of murder. I don't think I can ever forgive myself for that."

"Did Davenant hint to you at all that he meant to see Brotherhood about it?"

"No, never; he said there was still hope that my husband would stick to his word like a decent man."

"There's one other question I want to ask you, a rather odd one. Have you any reason to think that Davenant was carrying a golf-ball in his pocket when he came up on Tuesday afternoon?"

"He might be, of course. But he would hardly have mentioned it; would he?"

"No: only I had a special reason for asking. Well, Miss Rendall-Smith, I'll do my best, and if I want any more information I suppose I can come over and see you. Are you on the telephone?"

"Yes; it's Binver 35. Thank you so much, Mr. Reeves; I shall expect great things of you," and he showed her out, still smiling encouragement.

"That's a damned fine woman," he said to himself as he shut the door after her.

CHAPTER XVII

BY WHICH TRAIN?

H E met Marryatt on his way upstairs—Marryatt looking pained, as he always did when bad news went round.

"I must congratulate you on your driving, Reeves. It's all over the Club. But when I think of that poor fellow Davenant—I wonder now, do you think perhaps the jury will find Davenant was insane? Why do we always assume it's a madman's act to take one's own life, when it's surely a far more desperate thing to take anybody else's? Did you think, from what you saw of Davenant, that he was in mental health?"

"My dear Marryatt," said Reeves, "you're jumping to conclusions again. The police have arrested Davenant, because his movements since the time of the murder have been suspicious, and he has got to account for them. But there isn't any positive case against him as far as I know."

"I'm afraid the facts are only too clear," said Marryatt, shaking his head. "A man doesn't conceal himself so carefully unless there's a guilty conscience behind it. But I still ask myself, was it a sane man's act?"

Reeves was a little disappointed to find the assumption of Davenant's guilt so universal. People, he felt, were confoundedly illogical. He went to look for Carmichael, in the hope that he might have some new illuminating theories, but Gordon discouraged him.

"Carmichael says he's sick of the whole thing, and he's going back to golf. He speaks quite vindictively of Davenant, and really, I think, wants to see him hanged for not having been Brotherhood after all. It's an odd thing, human nature."

"Well, look here, Gordon, I've been seeing Miss Rendall-Smith, and she's been giving me a whole lot of information. Come and sit in my room for a bit, and let me get it clear; then we can think the case out all over again."

Gordon was not impressed by the recital of Miss Rendall-Smith's disclosures. "It seems to me," he said, "that every word of that makes the case against Davenant stronger instead of weaker. The one thing we had still to look for was a motive, and here's a motive ready-made. Davenant had every temptation to want Brotherhood out of the way; it would rid the world of a worm, and leave the course clear for him to marry the widow. I hope she won't go and tell all that story to the counsel for the defence."

"But what impressed me," objected Reeves, "was this—nobody knew more clearly than Miss Rendall-Smith what temptation Davenant had had to commit the murder, and yet nobody could have been more positive about Davenant's innocence. What I mean is this: isn't the strength of the *prima facie* evidence for his guilt the strongest possible test of her belief in Davenant's innocence?"

"*Credo quia impossibile*, you mean? Well, personally, I don't attach very much importance to the lady's feelings."

"I think that's very inconsistent of you, Gordon. Only the other day you were saying you would rather trust the evidence of people than the evidence of things."

"But her feelings aren't evidence. I'm willing enough to trust in what she knows about Davenant; but I'm not willing to trust in what she says she thinks she has persuaded herself to think she knows about Davenant. And that is about the correct description, I should say, for a woman's intuition."

"Oh, come! You must have a little more imagination than that."

"Well, look here, she says she trusts her intuitions, and wants you to trust them. She says she always does trust them and they never fail her. Now, this is the woman who, with her eyes open, went and married a dirty little sharper like Brotherhood. If women's intuitions were worth anything, wouldn't she have had an intuition which told her she was throwing herself away on a nasty little worm?"

"Well, let's leave her intuitions alone. I want to start

out with an absolutely unbiased mind, with no presumption for Davenant or against him. And I want you to help me to go through all the evidence we collected, and see if we can't make sense out of it somehow. Because we haven't done that yet, Davenant or no Davenant."

"You mean you want to do some thinking aloud, while I sit opposite you and say 'My dear Reeves! How on earth . . .' from time to time? All right; start away."

"Well, look here, what was the most incongruous thing we found, when we examined Brotherhood's body?"

"You mean me to say the two watches. To my mind it's the fact of his having a ticket. Because he surely had a season?"

"He did. I went and asked specially at the booking-office. But of course he might have left his at home by mistake."

"Yes, but that won't really do. Because on a line like this, surely, the porters know most of the season-ticket holders by heart? And the odds are that if he'd said, 'I've left my season at home,' the porter would have touched his cap and said, 'Right you are, sir.' Now, knowing that possibility, that all-but-certainty, was Brotherhood fool enough to go and book before he left London? As far as I remember, the tickets on this line aren't examined till you change or till you go out of the station."

"You're right. There's something that looks devilish wrong about that. Well, how did the ticket get there, then?"

"It looks, surely, as if it was put there after the man was dead."

"And if it was put there, it was put there to create a false impression, obviously. Now, let's see; what false impression could you create by putting a ticket in a dead man's pocket? That he was travelling on a different day—of course, that's possible."

"Yes, but that wasn't it: I mean, it wasn't on Monday that he was killed. Because he was seen going up on Tuesday morning; they said that at the inquest."

"Good, then that's excluded. Or you might create the impression that he was travelling third when he was really travelling first. But that would be useless, wouldn't it, because lots of people on this line travel first on a third-class ticket when the trains are crowded, and this train was. Or you might create the impression that he was travelling, when he wasn't really travelling at all. But Brotherhood clearly was, because he came up from London all right. The only other false impression would be that his destination was different from what it really was. But dash it all, his ticket was for Paston Whitchurch, and he was killed—Oh, good Lord!"

"What's the matter?"

"What fools we've been! Don't you see that if the man was really pitched out of the three o'clock from London, which doesn't stop between Weighford and Binver, a ticket for Paston Whitchurch would disguise the fact that he came by that train, and make everybody think he came in the later one —the 4.50 from Paston Oatvile?"

"By Gad, that sounds more promising. Then the murderer could prove an alibi by showing that he travelled on the three o'clock, eh?"

"That would be about the size of it. Let's see, had we any other reason for assuming the 4.50 train?"

"The watch—the wrist-watch, that is. It had stopped at 4.54."

"You mean that it stopped at a moment when its hands were pointing to 4.54. But obviously it would be the simplest thing in the world to fake a watch. And—I say, Gordon, we can prove it!"

"Prove it?"

"Yes, from the other watch, the stomach-watch. Don't you remember it was still going when we found it, only an hour fast? Well, the reason why it was an hour fast was that the murderer, at 3.54 on Tuesday afternoon, deliberately took it out of the pocket and turned it on to 4.54."

"You mean . . ."

"I mean that the murderer naturally assumed it would stop, like the wrist-watch. And if it had stopped, it would have registered 4.54, like the wrist-watch. But by the accident of its not stopping, we can prove what the murderer did!"

"I say, this is a day! but I feel as if there was something else we were held up over about the time —oh yes. Look here, we've now got to explain why Brotherhood ordered himself a sleeper for Wednesday, although one would have expected him to want to clear out on Tuesday. Our explanation, you see, was that coming to Paston Whitchurch on the 4.50 would make it too late for him to get a sleeper that night. But apparently we were wrong, because he came on the three o'clock from London; and I remember, when I looked it up in the time-table, I found he could have caught his train at Crewe—going on from Binver, of course."

"Yes, that's true. Still, it's only a subsidiary point. Let's see . . . the sleeper had originally been dated for the Thursday, hadn't it; and then Thursday had been scratched out and Wednesday put instead?"

"Yes, but it was no good supposing *that* was a fraud. Because Thursday wouldn't be any more probable than Wednesday,—in fact, less."

"Yes; it's confoundedly queer. I suppose he couldn't possibly—Gordon, what date was the Wednesday?"

"The 17th."

"It was? Then the Tuesday would be the 16th, and the Thursday the 18th."

"My dear Reeves! How on earth . . ."

"Child's play, my dear Gordon. No, but look here, it's serious. Don't you see that if there's one day of the week whose name can be easily changed to another it's Tuesday, which you can always change to Thursday?

And that if there's one number which can be easily changed it's 6, which you can always change to 8?"

"Yes, but this wasn't a change of . . ."

"Oh, don't you see? The sleeper was for Tuesday the 16th, the day of the murder. Brotherhood meant to go straight from Binver. The murderer found this sleeper-coupon in his pocket, and saw a golden opportunity of clinching his faked evidence about the trains. He could have destroyed the document, of course,—it was dangerous to him, because it proved that Brotherhood was really on the fast train. But he could do better by faking that too; changing Tuesday into Thursday and 16 into 18. Look here, how easy it is to do . . . There! Very little risk of detection there. But there was just a slight risk of detection, and this man wasn't taking any risks. So, having changed Tuesday the 16th into Thursday the 18th, he deliberately crossed out Thursday the 18th, and wrote in 'Wednesday' the '17th.' Double bluff, that is. People don't look for two corrections where they can see that there's one."

"I say, this murderer is some fellow!"

"Some fellow, but that fellow's name isn't Davenant. Don't you see, we've got the porter's word for it that Davenant came up from London by the later train, the 3.47. And Miss Rendall-Smith can also witness that he took the later train. So that, long before Davenant had got as far as Paston Oatvile—actually, when he was only seven minutes out of London—Brotherhood was falling down that embankment. And where's your conviction now?"

"Quite true—if we're right. But it is only cir-cumstantial evidence, isn't it? We've proved our own case more plausible than the case against Davenant, but we haven't shown that the case against Davenant is impossible. However, if we're right, one thing is pretty clear—that the murder was a deliberate one, deeply and carefully planned. And we've got to find somebody who had the motive and the opportunity to carry out this very elaborate scheme."

"I know. The police will never look at our objections until they lead us to find the real man. The police always want to have a victim."

"And we can't show, can we, that it was impossible for Davenant to throw a man out of the 4.50 train?"

"We can show it's improbable. Remember how crowded the 4.50 always is, how crowded it was on the day when you and I travelled by it. The three o'clock train from London, of course, wouldn't be a bit crowded; people haven't started getting away from business by then—it's only for ladies who have been up to shop. One could secure privacy even in a third-class carriage on that train."

"But it's only circumstantial evidence still."

"There are two other things we want to get to work on; the washing-list, as we called it, though I'm pretty certain it's nothing of the kind, which we found on the back of the cipher, and the golf-ball which we found beside the line."

"We want a theory, too, about the cipher. I wonder if Davenant admits that he wrote that cipher? You see, it will be apt to tell against him. He knew that Brotherhood had made a promise, and was threatening to break it. So that the police will attach importance to a document which tells him that he will perish if he goes back upon his faith."

"Yes, if they find out about it. But do you suppose the police have read that cipher? I very much doubt it."

"Aren't you going to tell them about it?"

"I don't think so. I know what you'll say, you'll say that one should always tell the truth. But it isn't an easy thing, telling the truth. I know what the truth is—namely that Davenant is innocent. I know, therefore, that this post card was a side-issue, irrelevant to the true explanation. If I show the police the meaning of the cipher, it will fortify them in what I know to be a false impression. Therefore, aren't I serving the best interests of truth if I sit on the cipher and say nothing about it?"

"I wonder," said Gordon.

CHAPTER XVIII

THE HOLMES METHOD

WHEN they met at breakfast next morning, Gordon was in a chastened mood.

"I was thinking over our ideas last night in bed, and I see that it's all a wash-out. The thing doesn't work."

"Doesn't work?"

"No, there are two snags which seem to me hopeless. Look here, if Brotherhood was chucked off the 4.50 from Paston Oatvile, one can understand why Davenant should have got the wind up. He may have seen the thing happen; or he may have seen Brotherhood get in at Oatvile and found he wasn't in the train when it got to Whitchurch—that might make him think there was something wrong, even if he'd really nothing to do with it. But if Davenant came back on the 4.50, and Brotherhood had been chucked off the earlier train, how did Davenant know anything about it? He would hear nothing, till he heard that we had found a dead body on the lines, and even then we weren't certain till next day whose body it was. Why did Davenant disappear, in that case, and hide in a very uncomfortable passage?"

"I thought of that. But you forget, Davenant was just coming back from an interview with Miss Rendall-Smith. He had probably seen her off on the three o'clock, and seen Brotherhood get into it. He comes down to the Hatcheries with the definite idea of remonstrating with Brotherhood; his first act, therefore, is to call at Brotherhood's house, and ask for him. He gathers, in the course of Mrs. Bramston's opening address, that Brotherhood has never turned up at all. Clearly, then, Brotherhood has either committed suicide or (more probably) vanished. In either case he has disappeared, and Davenant is afraid that he himself or (worse) Miss Rendall-Smith may be involved in the inquiry. It may be all right, of course, but there is danger. So he hits upon a very ingenious plan—going back to the secret passage in which he played as a child, and overhearing, as one does overhear in the Club, all the local gossip. Safe from observation, he can form his conclusions and mature his plans. He lies low until the moment at which he realizes that Miss Rendall-Smith is involved in the inquiry; and then by two incautious actions he gives himself away."

"Well, I suppose all that's possible. But here's the other snag, which is even worse: that copy of Momerie's *Immortality,* with the marks at the side which clearly betrayed Brotherhood's ownership, was found at Paston Oatvile in the 3.47 from London. Now, how did Brotherhood manage to leave his book in the 3.47 if he didn't travel in it?"

"That's true. But mightn't it be a blind? Remember, we're dealing with an extraordinarily clever criminal. He faked the ticket; he faked the watches; he faked the sleeper-coupon: mayn't he have managed to fake Brotherhood's train-literature as well?"

"We're dealing with a clever man, but not with one who's clever enough to come up here by the three o'clock, simultaneously leaving a book lying about in the 3.47."

"No, that's true; it does seem difficult. But there must be some explanation, mustn't there? Wait a minute . . . I know! When Carmichael got that book from the porter, the porter said he had taken it *off that train*. But a porter, when he says 'off the 3.47' doesn't necessarily mean 'off the 3.47 on Tuesday'—the day you are asking about. The 3.47 is to him a single entity which renews itself from day to day. He took that book off the train on Monday, depend upon it. Brotherhood left Momerie in the train when he came down on the Monday afternoon; consequently, Brotherhood probably never read the cipher that would have warned him of his danger. It wasn't till Friday that Carmichael made inquiries about the book, and of course by that time the porter wouldn't be able to remember, even if he tried, which *day* it was that the book was found."

"There's sense in that. I don't like it, though, I'm hanged if I do."

The hour after breakfast on Sunday was an hour of suspended animation in Paston Oatvile dormy-house.

Very few of the members ever went to church, and fewer than ever this week, when several of them had "kept a roller" (in Oxford parlance) by attending Brotherhood's funeral. On the other hand, it was not considered good form to start on the morning round until the padre had set out for the half-past nine service. Until that moment you smoked, read the Sunday papers, and in general tried to cultivate the air of a man in two minds as to whether he should go to church or no. The weather prospects were anxiously forecast; the political situation was greeted with apoplectic comments from the older members, and the Club acrostician went to and fro eliciting items of expert knowledge from anybody who was available. The atmosphere was one of Sabbath peace, yet the kind of peace that can only be secured by preparing for golf. Gordon had decided to take a rest from detection, and was intending to go round with Carmichael: Mordaunt Reeves was determined not to touch a club until the Links Mystery should be solved.

"If it comes to that," said Reeves, as they went upstairs, "have you considered this side of the question? A book cipher is ordinarily prearranged between the two parties. Now, in this one it is very unlikely that it was prearranged, for the message looks as if it came from an enemy. Therefore the message could only be sent by some one who knew that Brotherhood was reading Momerie's *Immortality* at the moment—knew, in fact, that the book was close to his hand. Well, how could Davenant know all that? He had not seen Brotherhood, he had not travelled with him—how was he to know that his thoughts would instinctively turn towards that particular book? For Davenant, it's impossible. What we want to find is somebody who knew that Brotherhood would have access to that particular book at that particular moment."

"Let's have another look at the book, anyway. Carmichael said that it was obviously Brotherhood's copy, because of the queries and things in the margin, but we haven't even verified that yet."

"They were met by an almost uncanny repetition of Reeves' experience two days before. He had put the paper-bound volume—he was positive that he had put it—in a particular place on his shelves. It was not there, and no amount of search in his rooms could discover it. In despair they sent for Carmichael, to know if for any reason of his own he had resumed possession of what, after all, was his book. He knew nothing of the disappearance; and was inclined to suspect deliberate theft. "You see," he said, "we never proved that it was Davenant who took away that cipher. We suspected him, of course, when we found that he had been hiding in the secret passage; the exchange of photographs can only be put down to him. But it's perfectly possible that the cipher was taken away by somebody who simply walked in at the door—somebody who is still in a position to walk in at the door and steal your books, Reeves."

"And that somebody isn't Davenant. Davenant, poor fellow, is under lock and key."

"It's a rum thing about that cipher," said Gordon. "When we've got it it doesn't seem to help us in the least, but whenever we want to get at it, it always seems that the important document has disappeared."

"It's getting on my nerves," admitted Reeves. "Seems to me I can't leave my room without something queer turning up."

"Look here, Carmichael," said Gordon, "this is where you come in. Get out your stethoscope and go down on all-fours and find clues for us."

"I am afraid that a person entering a room and taking a book away does not commonly leave very much mark on the surroundings. Let's take a look round, by all means—it's Sunday, after all, and the housemaid won't have been dusting. Maids, you will notice, always polish the grates on Sunday but do not dust the rooms; why, I cannot say. Whereabouts did you put the book, Reeves?"

"On that shelf there, the top but one."

"It was natural for you to put it there, because it's within your reach. But you're tall—I wonder if the other gentleman was shorter? I think a chair would be useful here . . . . Thank you. Yes, he was a good deal shorter. He had to stand on tip-toe to reach the book, and balanced himself, as we all do in such circumstances, by resting the four finger-tips of his left hand on the edge of the shelf beneath. In that way, you see, he could get the forefinger of his right hand on the top of the book. I should say he was a man of about Gordon's height."

"Unmasked!" cried Gordon, recoiling dramatically. "Send for the Black Maria; I'll go quiet."

"I was about to observe, my dear Gordon, that I attach no suspicion to you, because you have unusually long arms for your height. But this man, on the usual calculations, would be about our height, or a little smaller. Now, I wonder if he poked about in the other shelves at all? Most people, when they are looking for a book, take out one or two of the other books in mere inadvertent curiosity. Extraordinary the fascination that books have. I am told that Whitewell, at Oxford, loses twenty pounds' worth of books a year by theft, as the result of letting people prowl round his shop at it pleasure. Ah! Reeves, your room is an excellent subject for the detective."

"Why mine, particularly?"

"Because you are a man of such tidy habits."

"Tidy!" protested Gordon. "Look at those letters on the table."

"Pernickety would perhaps have been the just word. You are the sort of man who cannot leave a thing lying on the floor, he must pick it up. Consequently, you are the kind of man who always keeps his books on a dead level: some people do, some don't. Now, if this Shakespeare had been protruding like that yesterday, you would have noticed it and pushed it in."

"I suppose I should."

"Your visitor has not the same type of mind. He pushed in the two volumes on each side when he took it out, and then he put it back without driving it home, so to speak. Now, let's see if we can find which part he was reading. Ordinarily, as you doubtless know, if you open a book at random it will open at the page where it was last shut —that is, if it has been held open some little time . . . If that principle applies here, our unknown friend has been reading *Hamlet*—'To be or not to be' comes on this page."

"A rather banal taste," suggested Gordon. "You can't get much out of that."

"It suggests at least that he was a seriously minded person, and not all our fellow-residents are that. By the way, I suppose there is no chance that the secret passage is still being used?"

"Hardly. You see, it made me nervous, so I put that settee in front of it."

"One could push that out," suggested Gordon.

"But not put it back in position again once you were inside the passage. No, I think it must be a member of the club (just possibly a servant) we are looking for, who stands about five foot four and has sombre tastes in literature. Has he left any other traces? The fireplace is the only hope. Ah! He seems to me to treat you rather familiarly, Reeves—he has borrowed a pipe-cleaner and used it." And Carmichael, stooping, picked one out of the fireplace. "Did you have a fire yesterday?"

"No, life was too hurried. But I had one the day before."

"Then your grate was cleaned yesterday morning, not this morning. This pipe-cleaner is very dirty, which shows that your visitor did not, like yourself, wrap up his tobacco in those irritating little circles of paper which destroy all the taste. Gordon, you use them too, don't you? This was a stranger, then, though not necessarily the same who took the book. I think he came here yesterday, not this morning."

"Why?"

"Because the first pipe of the day is seldom foul; it has dried in the night. This was thoroughly foul. Of course, if the person who used this pipe-cleaner was the person who took the book, it's obvious he did not come in with any felonious intentions, or he would hardly have made himself so much at home."

"But that might have been a sudden idea."

"Of course. But I should be careful how you accuse people of theft merely because their pipes are newly cleaned. Let us just see if he emptied out his pipe first; if it was a plain tobacco, it will have left a Bottle . . . . Yes, here it is—as I feared, the inevitable Worker's Army Cut; half the Club smokes that. No, I'm afraid we can't put the handcuffs on anybody just yet. But, of course, you might find an excuse for going round your friends' rooms and looking for the lost book."

"During evening church," suggested Gordon,—

cynically, it is to be feared, for the function did not noticeably attract the Club members.

"Well, it all wants thinking out. You and Gordon had better go and play your round, while I see if I can make anything of it."

CHAPTER XIX

MORDAUNT REEVES TALKS TO HIMSELF

FOR some time after they had left, Mordaunt Reeves sat in his arm-chair hunting that most difficult of quarries, an intellectual inspiration. Merely artistic inspiration greets us when it wills, at the sight of a flower or of two lovers in a lane—we cannot chase it or make it come to our call. A merely intellectual problem can be solved by will-power, by sitting down to it with a wet towel round your head. But there are moments in an intellectual inquiry when inspiration can only come to us from dogged envisaging of the facts. Such was the point at which Reeves found himself; his clues were sufficient to exonerate, in his own mind at least, the arrested Davenant; they were not yet positive enough to mark out any victim who could be substituted. "A golf-ball," he kept saying to himself, "a golf-ball by the side of the railway line, a few yards behind the spot from which the murdered man fell. It must have something to do with it, but where, where does it fit in?" At last, weary of cudgelling his brains over the unlighted grate, he seized his cap and strode out into the air. Half of set purpose, half under the fascination of his thoughts, he found himself climbing once more the steep path that led up the railway embankment and on to the forbidden precincts of the line.

St. Luke's summer still held; the comparative silence of man's Sabbath conspired with the autumn stillness of nature—the sunshine quiet that is disturbed no longer by clicking grasshoppers, nor yet by cawing rooks—to hush the countryside. Far below him he could see the golfers at their orisons, fulfilling, between hope and fear, the daily cycle of their existence. Gordon and Carmichael were at the third tee now; he could have waved to them. Carmichael always made too much business about addressing the ball. Over there was the neglected house, itself radiating the silence of a forgotten past. All else was drowsing; he alone, Mordaunt Reeves, strode on relentlessly in pursuit of crime.

He threw himself down at full length on the bank, just beneath the line. "Now," he said, talking to himself out loud, "you are in the fast train from London to Binver, Mordaunt Reeves. It has stopped only once at a station, Weighford; probably oftener outside stations, because it is a foggy day and the trains get through slowly, with little fog-signals going off at intervals. If you fired a pistol at a fellow-passenger, it would probably be mistaken for a fog-signal by the people in the next carriage. Is that worth thinking of, I wonder? No, there must have been traces of a wound if a wound had been made, and it would have come out at the inquest. So you can't get much further that way, my dear.

"There is somebody in the train you badly want to murder. You want to murder him to-day, because his bankruptcy has just been declared, and if he is found dead people will think it is suicide. You have warned him to look out for himself—I wonder why you did that? But of course you must have done it on Monday so as to give him a chance to save himself. . . . No, that won't do, because you didn't know anything about his bankruptcy before Tuesday. . . . But the message reached him on Tuesday morning. That is to say, you have a motive for killing him which is probably quite unconnected with his bankruptcy, which is not known about at present— certainly kind Mr. Davenant does not know about it. He is not coming by this train, he is waiting till the 3.47. You sent this man a message on Monday, containing a cipher which depended on a book which was in his possession, which you knew was in his possession— did you, perhaps, give him that book? It will be a nuisance to you later on, when it is found, and you will want to steal it.

"Meanwhile, the train is steaming on, and you must do something; you must get on with the murder. Is he in the same carriage, or in a different one? And if it's a different one, is there a corridor between? Let's see, there's a corridor on the three o'clock train, but it doesn't connect with the slip that comes off at Binver. Probably you are in the Binver slip, because the railway people always try to shove one into that. I am sure you were in the slip, not in the corridor part of the train, because later on you are going to execute certain complicated manoeuvres over a dead man's body, and it would be dangerous to do that if a man might look in and say 'Tickets please' at any moment. No, you must be in the slip, and unless you are in the same carriage, there is no connection between you and him except along the footboard. That is rather hard to climb along while the train is going; but of course in the fog it may not be going just at this moment. It may be being held up by those signals that are connected with the Paston Whitchurch goods siding, those you see over there—at least, no, you do not see them because of the fog.

"But are you in the same carriage? You might have the decency to tell me that. Preferably not, because people saw you getting in, and people might remember afterwards that you got into the same carriage with him. Besides, you are choosing for the murder a part of the line where it curves, and curves away from the side where you are going to throw the man out. Why did you choose that particular part, unless you wanted to do something in the way of climbing along the footboard? I think you are in a different carriage. And you've got to murder somebody who is next door. Now, it's no good telling me that you're going to climb along the footboard and attack him, because he would certainly ring the communication cord if you did.

"He is alone in his first-class carriage, and you are alone in yours. Possibly he is asleep, but if so you've no means of knowing. You might, of course, bore a hole between the two carriages—and then? Put a cobra through, like the Speckled Band, to make him jump out of the train, or to kill him as he sits there? Not very probable, I think; cobras are so difficult to buy, as you rightly observe, without attracting suspicion. Or could you let loose some poisonous gas through the hole? That is a really bright idea; I give you 90 per cent. for it, only I hardly think a very practicable solution, my dear Reeves, if you don't mind my saying so. You would look such a fool getting into the train with a couple of oxygen cylinders, or a large balloon. No, you can't do anything with holes in the partition. To do anything, you must be leaning out of the window. If anything is to be done, you must both be leaning out of the window.

"Of course people do lean out of the window when the train stops and there isn't a station there. But you can't be certain that your man will look out: and people generally look out in the direction in which the train is curving: they can see more that way. And you could only make him look out—steady on! Keep steady, Reeves! Oh yes, you could certainly do that: thank you very much indeed; the whole thing becomes a good deal clearer. And then you hit him a good smack on the head, that stuns him anyhow, with a stick. That must have made you rather noticeable, because people don't take sticks up to London much—strong sticks, I mean. It would have to be—well, I'm blessed!"

And in another moment Reeves was scrambling down the bank, precipitous as it was, to a clump of rank grass some ten feet below. Half-hidden in this he had seen, and now painfully secured, a large knotted stick such as may be carried by a peaceable man, but undoubtedly would come in useful in a scrap. It might be coincidence of course, but that seemed too good to be true. And yet, was it not also too good to be true that he, nearly a week after the event, should be holding between his hands the very weapon, undiscovered hitherto, which had begun the assault? There was no name on it. There was no blood on it, nor any mark of violence. And yet it could undoubtedly have given a stunning blow without breaking or showing signs of the contact.

The next point was to get his treasure home, and this was not so easy as it sounds. He did not dare to carry it openly with him to the dormy-house; if the murderer really lived there he might easily catch sight of the stick and take the alarm. To carry a stick up your trousers-leg makes you a marked man at once. He left it concealed in the bushes a little way from the dormy-house, and went to fetch his golf-bag, in which he bestowed it upside down, and so smuggled it unobserved to his room.

Gordon and Carmichael were properly thrilled by the discovery, but were not very helpful in making suggestions for its use. Carmichael said that he might take the stick to Brotherhood's grave and see if it bled there, but added that this test was no longer used, he believed, in the detective world. On the whole, it seemed best to hide it away, taking no risks with stray visitors, and keep it until suspicion was thrown on some definite person—then it might come in handy. Meanwhile, Reeves thought he had now sufficient grounds for optimism about his case to justify him in a Sunday afternoon call on Miss Rendall-Smith. This time, Gordon refused to accompany him, and he went over in his own car, though he was careful to garage it at the hotel, for fear the sight of it might have painful memories for his hostess. There was no mistaking the eagerness and anxiety of the tone in which she asked for news. Reeves, with an indiscretion which he would have been the first to criticize a week ago, told her all his suspicions and all his hopes.

"You're a genius, Mr. Reeves," she said when he had finished.

"I'm afraid it's Carmichael that does all the clever work," he admitted. "Only it's so difficult to get him to keep up his interest in any subject, he always branches off to something else."

"It's most exasperating to think that I must actually have been on the same train with my husband, and not noticed anything," said Miss Rendall-Smith. "Now, let's see, which part of the train did I come on? Oh, it was the corridor part, I know, because I remember finding I had got into a smoker, and changing my carriage while the train was going. I was rather early for the train, so of course I shouldn't have seen anybody getting into the Binver slip behind."

"Did Davenant by any chance see you off?"

"Yes, he did."

"What sort of journey did you have?"

"Oh, we crawled. You know what this line is when there's a fog on. I never can see why there should be any danger, but we stopped at nearly all the signals. And now you mention it, I remember we did stop just at that curve of the line, a little way before Paston Whitchurch."

"You didn't see anybody you knew getting out of the train at Binver?"

"No, I didn't notice anybody. But then, I had to go to the Parcels Office about something, so I didn't go out with the crowd. Oh, it's maddening to think I've been so little use."

"Never mind, I dare say it might have put us off on a false scent if you had seen anybody."

"Mr. Reeves, I think I ought to tell you one other thing, though I dare say you will think it is just my fancy. I have a sort of feeling that I am being watched."

"Being watched?"

"Yes. When I took the train to come over to you yesterday, it was rather empty, as these Saturday trains are, and I noticed one of my fellow-passengers, a man who was quite a stranger to me. The curious thing was that he came back from Oatvile by the same train too, and I'm nearly certain, although this may have been just fancy, that I saw the same man watching me from the other side of the street when I went out this morning to go to church."

"This is rather serious. Do you know of anybody who had a grudge against you as well as against your husband?"

"Honestly, I can't think of anybody; you see, our lives have lain so far apart lately. No, I think it's probably just a coincidence; I was only going to suggest that, if I saw this man again, perhaps I might telephone to you?"

"Please do. Just send me word that you've seen him again and I'll come over straight in my car. Then perhaps we shall be able to have a better look at him."

Reeves drove away very thoughtful. Was it possible that the same enemy who had murdered her husband was on the widow's track too? Or was she psychic, and did echoes of the dead man's personality follow her? Certainly one might have expected Brotherhood to rest unquietly in his grave. His grave—would some fresh inspiration come to Reeves, perhaps, if he paid a visit to the grave in Paston Oatvile churchyard? He was half ashamed of the thought, and yet . . . it could do no harm.

The evening was a fine one; there was no need to be back early at the dormy-house. Instead of taking the London road, which was the shortest way home, he struck out along the winding country lane that connected the two Pastons. In a few minutes he had drawn up at the lych-gate, and was finding his way among the grave-stones.

The sudden gasp of a harmonium surprised him—of course, they were at evening service. What was that tune? "Nearer, my God, to Thee," wasn't it? He went up to the porch; it is an almost irresistible temptation to listen when sound comes out from a building into the open . . . . Yes, that was the hymn, most rustically sung by a congregation that sounded chiefly female, but with the one inevitable male voice dominating all, very loud and tuneless. Here in the porch you got a sort of quintessential effect of Sunday evening service in a country church: the smell of oil lamps, a glimpse of ugly deal pews, Sunday clothes, tablets on the wall in memory of dead virtues and hypocrisies. Yes, it was finishing now:

> So with my waking thoughts
>   Bright with Thy praise,
> Out of my stony griefs
>   Beth-hel I'll rai-haise.
> So by my woes to be
> Nearer, my God, to Thee,
>   Nea-rer-er to Thee————

and then the penetrating Amen for which the best efforts of the singers seemed to have been reserved. There was a rustle and a shuffling as the erect forms became sedentary, and then, with sudden clearness, Marryatt's voice giving out the text.

There was no doubt what Marryatt was at—it seemed a very embarrassing theme he had chosen. He was working up his congregation to derive a lesson from the tragic suddenness of Brotherhood's end; in the midst of life, he reminded his hearers, they were in death; thence he would proceed to refute Brotherhood's own arguments of less than a fortnight ago as to the survival of human personality. It was a thoughtful sermon, but on sufficiently obvious lines. "We see around us a great deal of carelessness, a great deal of indifference, a great deal of positive unbelief, and we ask ourselves, do we not? whether after all the lessons we learned at our mother's knee were not just old wives' fables, good for us when we were children, but something that manhood would outgrow. We ask ourselves, do we not? whether after all the story of our life will be continued elsewhere, whether after all there is a crown to be gained. And we persuade ourselves, perhaps, or think we have persuaded ourselves, that there is nothing beyond, nothing eternal that we can strive for. Death will be a quiet sleep, to just and to unjust alike, nothing but a sleep. And then the old questioning comes back to us:

> To sleep—perchance to dream; aye, there's the rub!
> For, in that sleep of death, what dreams may come
> When we have shuffled off this mortal coil
> Must give us pause

And so we see that our difficulties are not so easily
disposed of; that it is not so easy for us, after all, to get
the better of our alarms. . . ."

But Mordaunt Reeves heard no more of the sermon.
He was back in his car, on the road to the dormy-house,
and as he drove he talked to himself once more: " 'To be
or not to be'—well, I'm damned!"

CHAPTER XX

PROOF AT LAST

REEVES went to sit in Gordon's room when he got back; his own was apt to be a port of call for stray comers, and he wanted this to be a *tête-à-tête*.

"I wish to God," he started, "that I'd never been dragged into this beastly thing at all."

"Getting a brain-storm over it? Much better take to golf again; there's no sense in worrying over a problem that won't be solved."

"I have solved it."

"What!"

"I have solved it, and I wish to God I hadn't. Look here, Gordon, I know who it was who came into my rooms and took out my Shakespeare. It was Marryatt."

"Yes, but you don't mean———"

"It was Marryatt who took out my Shakespeare; he wanted to look up a quotation for his evening sermon. I know what you'll say—it was somebody else who took the Momerie. But it wasn't; I've been into Marryatt's room, and I found it there."

"Good Lord! Lying about?"

"It was on his table, but entirely covered with

papers—I thought, purposely. I didn't like doing it, but I felt the obvious thing was to look through those papers on Marryatt's table. Among them was a postcard from Brotherhood, dated a week ago, thanking him for the gift of a copy of Momnerie's *Immortality*."

"But, look here, the thing's impossible! Marryatt, I mean, Marryatt isn't the least the sort of person——"

"Yes, I know all that. I've thought of all that. But just look at the facts. There's not the least doubt it was Marryatt who came into my room, yesterday afternoon, I suppose. He came in, no doubt, for the pipe-cleaner or for the Shakespeare quotation—I don't grudge him either. Then he must have seen the Momerie on the shelf, and I suppose couldn't help taking it; he didn't feel safe as long as the thing was in my hands. He is, of course, just the height Carmichael mentioned; he does smoke Worker's Army Cut; his pipes always are foul."

"Yes, but he may have wanted the Momerie for anything."

"Why did he never tell me he'd taken it? Look here, you've got to face the facts. Let me marshal them for you; you can imagine I've been thinking them out pretty furiously. First, Marryatt had a reason for disliking Brotherhood."

"For disliking him, yes; but not for wanting to murder him."

"Of course to you and me it wouldn't seem so; we don't know the clerical temper from the inside. After all, Marryatt has a hard time of it in any case, trying to knock a little piety out of these villagers. What must he think of the man who comes and tries to take away what beliefs they've got?"

"All right, go on. Of course, it's quite impossible."

"Next point: it was Marryatt who gave Brotherhood that Momerie book. Brotherhood, of course, took it up to London with him in the train on Monday, but is it likely that anybody would notice it particularly? The one man who knew for certain that it was in his possession was the man who had given it to him."

"But did Marryatt know anything about Brotherhood's connection with Miss Rendall-Smith —about his promise to her?"

"We'll come to that presently. It doesn't arise yet, if you consider the actual wording of the cipher-message. What it said was, 'You will perish if you go back upon your *faith'*—I now read that as a purely theological message, and I know of only one man in the neighbourhood who would have been likely to send such a message."

"You seem to be pressing words rather far."

"Next point: Marryatt did travel by the three o'clock train on Tuesday. He made no secret of the fact; he told us about it—why? Precisely because he had arranged the murder so as to look as if it was connected with the 3.47: the three o'clock train was his alibi, and he was determined to get his alibi well rubbed in. Don't you remember, just before we found the body, the discussion we all had in the smoking-room about crime, and how Marryatt said it was very important for the criminal to behave naturally in company, so as to establish his alibi? Well, that's what he was doing at the moment."

"I'd forgotten his saying that."

"It doesn't do to forget these things. You've probably forgotten that it was Marryatt who started the whole subject, by saying it was the kind of afternoon when one would want to murder somebody. You see, he couldn't get the subject out of his mind, and he thought the easiest way to get it off his chest was to start talking about murder, quite naturally, in an abstract sort of way."

"You're making him out a pretty cool customer."

"He was, up to a point. Remember, he started out on a round, knowing that the body of his victim lay under the railway arch. Only at the third tee his nerve deserted him, and he pulled his drive."

"Yes, but hang it all, anybody——"

"I'm only mentioning the fact; I don't say there was necessarily anything significant about it. Anyhow, I sliced mine, and so we came to find Brotherhood's body. And that was too much for him; you will remember that at the moment he was quite unnerved. We had to send him off to fetch Beazly—and he wasn't half glad to go. After that, remember, right up to the time of the inquest, he was in a state of pitiful agitation. He explained that by telling us that he was nervous about whether he'd be allowed to bury Brotherhood or not; but when you come to think of it, does that account for the extraordinary excitement and nervousness he showed about the whole thing? Anyhow, the jury found suicide—and remember, he always wanted us to believe it was suicide—and immediately his trouble vanished. He seemed to lose interest in the business from then on.

"But over one thing he did give himself away. Do you remember, when Carmichael produced that photo of Miss Rendall-Smith, Marryatt professed not to know who it was? Now, I fancy there are aspects of the case here which we haven't been able to trace yet. But on the face of it, it was curious that Marryatt, who has lived here for quite a long time and knows all the clerical society round here, shouldn't know the daughter of the man who used to be Rector of Binver. For some reason, he preferred not to be in the know. He said he'd take it over to Binver and identify it. He took it over: it was early-closing day, and Campbell's studio must really have been shut. But Marryatt comes back with some lame story about Campbell not being shut after all; and he tells us, not only whom the photograph represents, but the whole life-story of the lady into the bargain. I say, he made a mistake there. We ought to have been suspicious.

"We were not suspicious; he came and played bridge in my room the same night. It gave him a very nasty turn when, as we all thought, the photograph altered its appearance. He was completely unstrung; and the form his nerves took was an intense desire that we should drop the inquiry altogether. He had begun to grow superstitious, as so many murderers do. But he made the best use he could of it, by trying to shut down our investigations on the strength of it. That failed, but something even better turned up—Davenant's hiding in the secret passage. By the way, I'm pretty well convinced, though I can't prove it, that it was Marryatt and not Davenant who took away the copy of that paper, with the cipher on it. Of course, when we found Davenant, it not only concealed the fact that he had taken away the cipher, but also turned the suspicion into quite a different channel.

"Here, I must admit, Marryatt shows up badly. He saw an innocent man accused, and he took no action to exculpate him. On the contrary, he stated to me quite emphatically his belief in Davenant's guilt. But we mustn't judge him hardly; he may have meant—he may still mean, for all we know, to come forward if Davenant is found guilty. Meanwhile, there's one more piece of evidence which I understand now, though it has bothered us a good deal. You remember the thing we call the 'washing-list,' the words we found on the back of the anonymous letter?"

"Yes, rather. What about it?"

"Well, it clearly wasn't part of the cipher, was it?"

"Probably not—one can't be certain, but it didn't look like it."

"Well then, you've got to choose, it seems to me, between two possibilities. One is that this sheet of paper—it's only a half-sheet in any case—was blank until the cipher was written on it. Then it passed into Brotherhood's possession, and Brotherhood, looking about for a piece of paper to jot down a list on, found this one and used it."

"That's what I'd assumed."

"In that case, it's hard to see any special significance about the list, isn't it? It's not in Brotherhood's writing, apparently; but of course if he wrote it in the train, it's possible that his handwriting would be untraceable."

"What's the other possibility?"

"Why, just the other way round. That the list, whatever its meaning may be, was written on that piece of paper first. And then the murderer, wanting to send the cipher message to Brotherhood, took up that piece of paper at random to write it on, without noticing that there were already four words pencilled on the back."

"That's possible, certainly."

"Well, don't you see, in that case the list becomes very important, because it was written not by Brotherhood but by the murderer, and it may accidentally give us a clue to the murderer's character."

"A rather obscure clue. As far as I remember all it said was Socks, Vest, Hem, Tins."

"Yes, but look here: do you remember my asking whether those words were written on the paper, right at the edge of the paper, before or after the sheet was torn in half? Well, my own belief has always been that those are only parts of words, and that the other half, possibly with a lot more writing as well, was lost to us when the sheet was torn."

"And you've restored the full words?"

"I think I have. I'm just going to write it out for you." And, after scribbling for a moment, he put before Gordon two sheets of paper; one, which was blank, partly covered the other, so as to hide part of what had been written on it.

"Well, that's all correct," said Gordon: "Socks, Vest, Hem, Tins, all present. Do you want me to guess the other halves of the words—the first half, I suppose, in each case? Because I give you fair warning that I have never guessed a riddle in my life."

Reeves took away the upper sheet of paper, and made Gordon read again.

"Hassocks, Harvest, Anthem, Mattins—well, I'm blowed! You ought to be given a fountain-pen for this sort of thing."

"But seriously, isn't it almost certain that those were the words of the original, before the sheet was torn in half? What connected them, of course, we can't say. But they're all ecclesiastical words—at least, you can say that 'harvest' is an ecclesiastical word at this time of the year, with harvest festivals coming on. Could such a sheet of paper have been lying about and been taken up carelessly anywhere but in a clergyman's rooms? And honestly, doesn't that clinch the case against Marryatt?"

"Well, it certainly looks as if one would like to ask Marryatt a few questions. Though, mark you, I refuse to believe that Marryatt laid hands on Brotherhood."

"We can't ask him questions. We must put him to a test."

"What sort of a test?"

"Well, surely the stick might come in handy there. If we could somehow confront him with it suddenly, and see how he takes it—I believe they do that sort of thing in America."

"Carmichael, I fancy, would tell you that the system was originally Danish."

"Why Danish?"

"Really, Reeves, what is the use of all your researches into *Hamlet*, if you don't realize that your present idea is just what Hamlet does to the King and Queen when the Players come on? I think, you know, it's rather a dangerous method, because it's so easy to suggest things to a person's mind when they're not there already. But this I will say, if Marryatt recoils from the sight of that stick which you picked up this afternoon, or shows any trace of confusion when he sees it, then—I won't say I'll be prepared to regard Marryatt as guilty, but I'll be prepared to ask him for an explanation."

"Well, Sadducee, have it your own way. We'll put that stick and the golf-ball lying out prominently in my room. At dinner we'll ask Marryatt to come along afterwards. We'll go out of dinner early, and get into the secret passage. From there we can watch and see what happens when he comes in."

"Don't you think it would be a mistake to ask him in? It might somehow put him on his guard. . . . Yes, I know, I can make sure that he comes into your room without being asked. Leave that part to me, and stand by as soon as dinner's over. We can go up into the passage by the billiard-room end."

CHAPTER XXI

THE TEST

MARRYATT came and sat with them at dinner—a situation which called forth Reeves' utmost powers of self-control. He was glad that Carmichael was there too; glad that he had not communicated to him the suspicions which he had just come to entertain. He could not help admiring the easy way in which Gordon managed to conceal *his* suspicions, talking to Marryatt in his ordinary vein of rather pawky pleasantry.

"Well, Marryatt, how was the collection?" was the first sample of it.

"Normal, thank you. It's fortunate that I don't depend on it for my livelihood, or you would have to wait some time for that half-crown I owe you."

"And how was the choir on the top notes?"

"There and thereabouts," said Marryatt cautiously.

"Do you know," Carmichael put in, "there's a passage in Longfellow's 'Village Blacksmith' which has always seemed to me a curious example of amphibology. The blacksmith, if you remember, is said to go on Sunday to the church, where he 'hears the parson pray and preach,

he hears his daughter's voice singing in the village choir.'
The context shows that it is the blacksmith's daughter
who is alluded to, but by the ordinary rules of grammar
it ought to be the parson's daughter. I'm not much of a
church-goer myself——"

"Marryatt," continued Gordon, "do you have anthems
often in church?"

The word "anthems" made Reeves feel as if he had
leapt a foot into the air. Marryatt, however, showed no
traces of excitement.

"Very rarely, I am thankful to say."

"And those, I suppose, are at Evensong, not at
Mattins?"

Reeves frowned slightly. This effort to introduce the
significant words seemed to him painfully forced, and
at the same time quite useless. It was not likely that
Marryatt would connect the words on the "washing-list"
with the cipher he had inadvertently sent to Brotherhood
on the same sheet of paper.

"No, not at Mattins. The *Te Deum*, I am afraid,
exercises the capacities of my choir to their full limit."

"You just have them on big days, I suppose, like
Harvest Festivals?"

"That kind of thing. Really, Gordon, you seem very
ecclesiastical this evening. Were you going to offer to
sing in the choir or anything?"

"No, my boy, not till you get some more comfortable
hassocks."

"As a matter of fact, I have ordered some only lately. I have to go up to London to-morrow to see about them."

Reeves' blood thrilled. Only a tiny corroboration, and yet enough to give him more confidence in his diagnosis of the "washing-list." Only lately Marryatt had been ordering new hassocks—it all fitted in.

"I congratulate you, Marryatt," said Carmichael. "At the funeral the other day, I am afraid I found myself chiefly thinking about the unpleasantness of the kneeling accommodation, instead of the virtues of the deceased. By the way, have you declared a truce in the controversy with Brotherhood, now that he is no longer capable of replying?"

"I am afraid I continued the course this evening. I could not very well leave it where I had left off last Sunday. I had to meet, you see, his views about immortality."

Carmichael chuckled. "Well, let's hope Brotherhood won't walk," he said. "It would be very embarrassing for you, Marryatt, if Brotherhood's ghost came back to continue the discussion. It would speak with so much expert knowledge."

"Really, Carmichael," said Marryatt, "I wish you wouldn't say those things. You told us yourself that you don't believe in spiritualistic phenomena."

"It's all right," said Gordon, "you'll be able to exorcise him if he does turn up again. Try driving a stake through his body, I'm told it's effective. Hullo!" he added, consulting his watch, "I'd no idea it was so late. I promised I'd go and help Murdoch fix up his wireless. So long———" and he disappeared, giving a slight tug at Reeves' coat as he left.

He did not seem, however, to be in a hurry to redeem his promise. Instead, he made straight for Marryatt's room, taking the stairs three at a time; and his proceedings in Marryatt's room were sufficiently curious to be worth recording in detail. First, he took two out of the three pipes which lay there, and hid them carefully behind the coalscuttle. Then he pulled the remaining pipe in half; picked a strand or two of tobacco out of the nearest tin, and rammed these tightly down the stem of the pipe, close to the mouthpiece. There were a couple of feathers on the mantelpiece; these he unscrupulously put in his pocket. And, "Now, my friend," he said to himself out loud, as he left the room, "I think we've spiked your guns. I for one shall be surprised if you don't come along hunting for pipecleaners." And so he went down and rejoined Reeves in the deserted billiard-room.

The Committee had not yet decided what action to take about the secret passage, and it was with no difficulty that the two friends entered it again from the billiard-room end, and made their way along it, guided by Reeves' torch. If it had lost its thrill of human mystery, it had acquired instead a kind of impersonal dreariness. One had not looked for ghosts, when one was expecting a murderer to be lurking there; now, you caught your breath a little as you passed the hiding-hole. Priests had lain close here many times; strange irony, that it should now be serving as a vantage-point for spying on a clerical delinquent. There were two cracks in the panelling of Reeves' room, and through either you could see, in the shifting firelight, the dark outlines of the oaken cudgel that lay against Reeves' arm-chair. By a grim accident, it stood exactly as if it were being held in the right hand of some one seated there. It could not fail to catch the eye of anyone who turned on the electric light, when he came in.

Voices, echoed up the staircase, proclaimed the breaking up of the dining-tables. They could distinguish Carmichael's high-pitched accents, as he told an interminable story at the foot of the stairs —no doubt to Marryatt, who still delayed his coming. Then at last they heard Marryatt's step, the rather boyish, light step that characterized him; he was still crooning, if further identification were needed, the hymn Reeves had heard from the churchyard.

> Though, like a wanderer,
> The sun gone down,
> Darkness comes over me,
> My rest a stone,
> Still in my dreams I'd be——

and the sounds died away with the footfalls, as Marryatt turned the corner into his own room.

Then there was silence; a silence fraught with
expectation, and for Gordon with anxiety. Why hadn't
he come? Had he, after all—one ought to have considered
that—another pipe in his pocket? Had some splinter or
paper-clip succeeded in removing the all-important
obstruction? No; Marryatt's door was suddenly flung
open with an impatient gesture; Marryatt's step was heard
again in the passage; Marryatt's voice still found
occupation in rendering the hymn, but more savagely
now—you pictured a bear robbed of her whelps.

> There let my way appear,
>   Steps unto heaven,
>   All that Thou sendest me
>   In mercy given——

and at that the door suddenly swung open, and the
light was switched on.

> Angels to beckon me——

The voice stopped dead in mid-tone. There was a sharp,
nerve-wracking crash as a pipe fell on the floor-boards.
Marryatt was standing in the door-way as if transfixed,
staring at the oaken stick, his face distorted with terror.
Half in excitement, half in relief, Reeves drew a deep
breath, which came out with a slight whistle—he must
be careful not to do that again, or he might betray his

presence. . . . No, precaution was needless. Marryatt had turned; he strode in silence down the passage like a man pursued, and they heard his door shut behind him, the key turn in the lock.

Very cautiously, Reeves and Gordon pushed aside the settee which blocked the entrance of the passage, and stepped out into the room. Marryatt had left his pipe where it lay, had not turned off the light as he went out.

"Now," said Reeves, "what d'you make of Marryatt's innocence?"

"I'm going along to his room," said Gordon.

"No, look here, you mustn't do that. We haven't decided what we're going to say to him, what we're to do about it. Leave him alone for the present."

"I'm not going in," said Gordon. He tiptoed along the passage outside, till he came opposite Marrayatt's door, and stood irresolute. Then suddenly he heard a muffled voice from inside. "Oh, my God!" and again, "Oh, my God!" He tiptoed back again, his face grave. "Look here, Reeves, I can't understand it. I tell you, I can't understand it."

"It doesn't much matter whether we understand it or not; the point is, what to do about it?" We can have explanations later on. But I daren't go to a man and say, 'Look here, are you a murderer?' Besides, I know he is one. I can't simply tell the police what I know, and leave them to get on with it; it seems so mean. Besides, I don't think I want anything to happen to Marryatt. Only I've promised Miss Rendall-Smith that I'll do my best to get Davenant off. What am I to do?"

"If you feel like that—I suppose you wouldn't trust me to talk to him?"

"It's awfully good of you, but you know, I feel it's up to me. I must form my own conclusions."

"Then, if I were you, I'd write him a letter, simply pointing out that there are certain actions of his which you can't quite explain, and asking him to explain them. Tell him you're still worried over Brotherhood's murder, and feel that perhaps he may be concealing something, from whatever motive, which might lead you to the truth if you knew about it. Reeves, I'm sure the man isn't a murderer: you only want to get him to explain things."

"Yes, but the whole business hangs together. I can't tell him how I formed my suspicions without telling him the whole of the evidence I've got; and that means putting it to him straight out. I must see that he manages to exculpate Davenant; as long as he does that, I don't mind if he goes abroad—I don't mind giving him time to get away. But I must show him where he stands, and I must get a confession out of him."

"But the thing's impossible!"

"Look here, I've got it—the telephone! That lets you talk to a man without seeing his face, without letting him answer if you don't want him to; you can treat him as if he wasn't there. I know it sounds a silly dodge, but you see my idea, don't you?"

"I should have thought it would be rather public. Can't the people at the exchange overhear everything if they want to?"

"Yes; I'd forgotten that. I know—the speaking-tube in the steward's office! I can get the steward to let me have the use of the room for ten minutes in the slack time to-morrow morning. Then I'll call up to Marryatt and tell him all I want to."

"The trouble about that speaking tube is, it isn't really made for dialogue. I mean, you have to speak and listen alternately through the same tube."

"All the better. I don't want any interruptions from him. Now, a game of bezique for Heaven's sake: my nerves are all anyhow."

CHAPTER XXII

IN THE FOG

"HULLO, Marryatt, is that you?"

"Yes; who's speaking?"

"It's about Brotherhood. You'll guess before I've finished who it is speaking, so I'd better tell you at once; it's Reeves. I am going to talk to you for about ten minutes through this tube, and you'll see for yourself as I go along that it's to your own interest to hear me out to the end. I've chosen this way of speaking to you purposely, so as to save you the embarrassment of an interview. But, of course, it's no good your trying to interrupt, because I shouldn't hear if you did.

"I have managed to trace your movements during this last week pretty exactly, and I'm going to describe them to you, so that you can see how much I know, and how little use it is for you to try and put up any denial. Of course, I may make little mistakes about the details, but I think you'll find that there is not much wrong.

"I can understand you not liking Brotherhood; few of us did. But while the rest of us simply disliked him, you hated him. Whether you hated him before he began giving his atheist lectures I don't know. I dare say there was a quarrel beforehand and that was what made him give the lectures. Anyhow, when he started trying to undermine the beliefs of your parishioners, your hatred reached such a pitch that you determined to do away with him. I am not going to moralize about all that; I suppose you felt at the time that you were doing God's work, and you fortified yourself with precedents from the Bible. To you, perhaps, it was like crushing some noxious insect. I'm not going to argue morality.

"One characteristic scruple detained you. You did not shrink from undoing God's work by destroying the material body of the man you hated, but you trembled for the prospects of his soul if his life was thus suddenly brought to an end. You decided that you must warn him of the danger he ran, but how were you to warn him without risk of discovery? You sent him a present of a book about immortality; that seemed natural enough, as it was the subject he had been lecturing about. Then, anonymously, you sent him a message which consisted only of figures, yet so arranged that a clever man like Brotherhood could see that the figures were a cipher, and that this book was the key to the cipher. The message you sent ran, 'You will perish if you go back upon your faith.' Then you felt you had warned him sufficiently. As a matter of fact, he left the book in the train on Monday, and therefore your warning, which reached him on Tuesday, was in any case too late.

"Your alibi was brilliantly thought out beforehand.

You went up to London, being careful to tell us all that
you were going. You took with you no weapon except a
heavy stick. But you had a powerful ally in the grey fog
which hung over the railway line that day; the fog which
made the movements of the trains slow, their timing
uncertain, their carriages almost invisible from each
other. You had chosen your day well. You knew, I take
it, beforehand that Brotherhood's bankruptcy would soon
be public property; you took good care, anyhow, to
inform yourself of the fact when you got up to Town.
That meant that the way was clear for you; the murder
would be interpreted as suicide.

"You went up by the same train as Brotherhood; you
took care to come back by the same train. You shadowed
him, I suppose—easy work for you to do that unseen in
the grey fog. You saw him enter a carriage which was (I
think) the last of a coach. That was probably a
disappointment to you, because you could not take the
one immediately behind. No matter, you took the one
immediately in front instead. Each travelled first, and
each was alone in his carriage; it was not difficult to
secure that in such weather, on such an unfrequented
train. The whistle blew, and you went out into the fog.

"You could do nothing on the first stage of your
journey; it was necessary for you to reach ground that
you knew; you could not be certain, in the fog, that the
blow would be fatal if you struck it elsewhere. You waited
till the train got to the beginning of the Paston Oatvile

viaduct, and there, as you expected, it was held up by
the signals. That meant that you were just at the beginning
of the viaduct, so that a body falling over must necessarily
go to its destruction. It meant also, owing to the curve,
that the other coaches were all but out of sight from yours;
in any case, you were hardly visible in the fog.

"Then it was that you took out of your pocket a
golf-ball—a golf-ball of a very common kind, by which
you could not be traced. Leaning out of the window on
the left-hand side of the train, you threw the ball
backwards, in such a way as to hit the further window of
Brotherhood's carriage, the window on the side furthest
from the engine, I mean. Your idea was that the ball,
bouncing off with considerable speed, would fall into
the valley below, where of course it would arouse no
suspicion if it were found. As a matter of fact, it lodged
at the top of the viaduct and was there found by me.

"Brotherhood was startled at the noise, and, as you
had hoped, he put his head out of the window. As you
had hoped, he looked backwards in doing so, because it
was the back window that the ball had hit. At that moment
you brought down your stick with a violent blow over
his skull, and he must have fallen doubled up over the
window-frame.

"It was not difficult, with the train stationary and the
fog all around you, to climb along the footboard, still on
the left-hand side of the train. You had to be quick,
though, for the train might move on at any moment. You

removed his season-ticket, and substituted a third-class ticket for Paston Whitchurch. The train you were on did not stop at Paston Whitchurch; the ticket, then, would make people think that Brotherhood had fallen from the slow train that went past later. You changed the time of his watch, in order to confirm this impression. You put a wrist-watch on him, registering the same time, so as to make assurance doubly sure. There you over-reached yourself; there is no need to explain how.

"All this you did while your victim, I suppose, still breathed. And still the train was held up by the signals. There was time to search the pockets. Your cipher-letter was still in his pocket; you thought there was no need to destroy that, because its secret could not be penetrated. You forgot that on the back of the sheet of note-paper on which you sent the cipher message you had jotted down some references to anthems, mattins, and so on, which helped me ultimately to trace the crime to you. You also found a coupon for a sleeping-carriage; that, too, you did not destroy, but you altered the dates, because your quick brain saw that a sleeping-carriage coupon for Tuesday would not have been held by a man travelling in the later train, the 4.50.

"Then you took the living body and heaved it out of the carriage-window, over the viaduct. That was just as the train started, or when it had already started; it was a moment later that you saw you had left the dead man's hat in the rack, and threw that over too. One thing you allowed to fall over without meaning to—the stick with which you inflicted the first wound; it slipped, I suppose, from your hand: certainly it was found just on the edge of the viaduct, a few feet down the embankment. When you reached Binver you came straight back to us, and were careful to tell us that you had come back by the three o'clock train.

"You have had some bad moments since then —when I sliced my drive into the osiers, and found the body, and you had to look at your victim; when your superstitious fears made you think that a photograph had come to life; when you saw on my shelves, and stole from them, the very copy of Momerie's *Immortality* which you had given to Brotherhood: when, finally, you came into my room last night, and saw in front of you the stick with which the crime was committed. But what should have caused you more horror is the fact than an innocent man, Davenant, is awaiting trial on the charge of murder, and you have taken no steps, so far, to exculpate him. That I cannot understand, but I hope you meant to do so; certainly you will have to do so.

"I want you to write out a full confession of these facts, and to bring it to my room to sign it; I will witness it, and Gordon, to whom the facts themselves are already known. After that, you are free to go where you will. Respect for your cloth and for our friendship makes this the only possible course for us. Your confession will not be made public unless that is the only way of saving

Davenant from execution or a life sentence. Of course, we are taking a considerable risk ourselves——"

The door of the steward's office swung open, and Carmichael came in, saying as he turned the corner, "Hullo, Reeves, have you heard that Davenant has confessed? Oh, sorry, I didn't see you were telephoning."

CHAPTER XXIII

MARRYATT BREAKS THE PLEDGE

MORDAUNT REEVES looked up in a dazed way, still holding the tube. "What was that you said?"

"I said, Davenant's confessed. It's an extraordinary thing, you know, the way we use ambiguous expressions, and expect the other man to interpret them in the right sense. Davenant, now, is a Catholic, and therefore it's absurd for me to say 'Davenant's confessed' as if I were to rush into the room and say 'Davenant's shaved.' But when I say 'Davenant's confessed,' I mean, and expect you to understand me as meaning, Davenant has confessed *to the police that he murdered Brotherhood*."

"Marryatt, Marryatt!" Reeves held his ear to the tube, but no answer came. "Excuse me one moment, Carmichael; I must just go up and see Marryatt."

"Ambiguity again; do you mean upstairs, or up to London?"

"Upstairs, of course, why——"

"In that case, I'd better tell you that I met Marryatt, five minutes ago or thereabouts, running violently in the direction of the station."

"Running?"

"Yes. It was my conjecture that he intended to catch the 10.30, and had not very much time to do it in."

"Good Lord, this is awful! I say, have you seen Gordon?"

"He is just outside. He wanted me to do a round with him, but I found myself unable to comply. The fact is, my wife returns to-day, and I have to go down to the house to prepare for her—just see that the servants are not intoxicated, and that kind of thing. If you want a round, Gordon is your man."

"Thanks, I think that's just what I do want. Hullo, Gordon, you going out? Just let me get my clubs, and I'm with you."

It was not till they were walking together along the fairway from the first tee that Reeves opened his griefs. "I say, have you heard this about Davenant?"

"Yes, most inconsiderate of him to confess just when you'd arranged to clap the darbies on another man. Lucky for you you hadn't said anything to Marryatt about it."

"Well, the fact is, I had."

"You had?"

"Yes, I've just been talking to him from the steward's office, through that confounded metaphone thing. I told him the whole story, as we had put it together——"

"I pass the *we*."

"And I told him he must own up. He had no chance

of saying anything down the tube, of course, and now it seems he has bolted for London."

"Bolted! Why, of course, that was why he was making streaks for the station at about sixty miles an hour. Good Lord, Reeves, you have done it? I believe you've convinced Marryatt, by sheer logic, that he's a murderer, when he's nothing of the kind."

"No, but I say, do you really think he's bolted?"

"Looks like it, doesn't it? Very much like the old story of the man who telegraphed to the Bishop to say 'All is discovered; fly at once.' Poor old Marryatt must have a guilty conscience about something, mustn't he? I wonder if he's been embezzling the collections? I should think it would be worth about a fortnight in quod, embezzling the Paston Oatvile collections. My ball, I think."

"I wish you'd take this thing seriously."

"I'm doing my best; it was a beast of a lie."

"I don't mean the game, you fool, I mean Marryatt clearing off like this. What happens if he really tries to disappear? How am I to get at him? And what's it all about, anyhow?"

"I haven't the faintest idea what it's all about. But if you ask me, I don't believe Marryatt has bolted for good. He wasn't taking his clubs with him."

"You think he'll come back this evening?"

"I should think almost certainly."

"But look here, what the deuce am I to say to him when he does?"

"Oh, leave all that to me. I'll calm his fevered brow. I told you yesterday there were one or two little things I wanted Marryatt to explain, and you wouldn't let me. This time, I'm going to have it my own way."

"It's awfully good of you if you . . . Oh, Lord, right over the green, as usual . . . But, I say, tell me about Davenant. How did you hear?"

"The head waiter was the source of the information, but I gather it is on good authority. According to the gossip of Binver, the police were trying to incriminate your friend Miss Rendall-Smith, and that's how they got Davenant to own up. Dirty dodge, rather, I think."

"Trying to incriminate her? Then, of course, it was the police who were shadowing her! She told me yesterday she thought she was being watched."

"That would be it, I suppose."

"But then, how did Davenant explain all the things that have been puzzling us all this time?"

"I don't think he's been interviewed by the *Daily Mail* yet. But if you mean how he explained the difficulty about the two trains, that's very simple. It wasn't done from a train at all."

"Not from a train?"

"No. He was walking with Brotherhood along the railway line in the fog, and he lost his temper and pitched him over. At least, that's the story they're telling down at Binver."

"Oh, I see. That being so, this for the hole."

They went round again that afternoon. There was really nothing else to be done; but Reeves was in a pitiable state of suspense all the time, and the hours travelled slowly. The 3.47 put down its generous toll of passengers at Paston Oatvile, but no Marryatt among them. Two more trains came in, and still no Marryatt appeared: his place was empty at the dinner-table. Reeves was in terror that he might come back in the middle; in terror that he might not come back at all. At last, as they went out from dinner, they caught sight of his face, looking white and haggard, in the entrance hall. Reeves bounded upstairs, full of relief, while Gordon marked down his man.

"Hullo, Marryatt? Had dinner? Good; come and sit in the lounge for a bit. I'd been wanting to see you."

There was only one way to open the conversation. "Have a small something in the whisky line," he suggested.

"No, thanks. Knocked off."

"Knocked off! Why on earth? Are you going to start a Band of Hope? I'm sorry, Marryatt, but I'm afraid you won't get many members to join."

"No. It's nothing of that sort. Doctor's orders, you know."

"First time I ever heard of Beazly prescribing that."

"It wasn't Beazly. I've just been up to London, you know; I went to see a specialist."

"I say, I'm awfully sorry; what's wrong? Heart?"

"Well, it was a sort of nerve man I went to. Didn't seem to be much use. He talked to me for about half an hour about French cathedrals, and then told me to knock off drinking and smoking."

"Yes, but dash it all, what were your symptoms?"

"I say, Gordon, do you believe in—well, in ghosts and things?"

"Not more than's good for me. Why? You been seeing spooks?"

"Look here, I wanted to tell somebody about it. You know, of course, that I preached about Brotherhood last night. I wasn't quite sure whether it was the thing to do—it seemed a bit unfair at the time. Anyhow, I felt I ought to. Then at dinner, if you remember, you and Carmichael were ragging about it—wondering what would happen if old Brotherhood came back."

"Yes, I remember."

"Well, of course that may have preyed on my nerves a bit. Anyhow, I went upstairs to my room, and found my pipe shocked up—you know."

"Yes, it's funny the way they do get shocked up."

"So I went along to Reeves' room to bag one of his pipe-cleaners. It was dark and he wasn't in, so I turned on the light. And there, right in front of me, I saw old Brotherhood's oak stick—the one he used to carry with him, I remember, when he preached on the village green. I remember his quoting Johnson's refutation of

Berkeley—you know the thing—and banging that stick on the ground. That was the stick I saw."

"In Reeves' room?"

"Yes, by the side of his arm-chair. And—I didn't exactly *see* anything, you know, only it looked exactly as if Brotherhood himself were sitting in the chair, invisible, with his hand resting on the stick. I was just telling myself I was a fool, when—he breathed."

"Who did?"

"I don't know. There was nobody in the room— nobody visible, I mean. That was too much for me, I'm afraid. I went to my room and locked myself in. You see, I'm psychic, rather. Always have been, from a kid."

"And was that all your trouble?"

"No. I had half thought about seeing a man about it while I was up in London anyhow. And then, just as I was starting for the train, that beastly metaphone thing in my room whistled. So I went and said 'Who's speaking? '—and—I may be an awful fool, you know, but I thought the thing said 'It's Brotherhood.' And at that I fairly dropped the tube and raced for the train. Then in London I went to see this fool of a specialist, and of course he told me I'd been overdoing it."

Gordon's eyes twinkled. "You'd have saved yourself a couple of guineas at least," he said, "if you'd talked to me earlier."

"Oh! Why, what's the point?"

"Well—that stick. It had a perfect right to be in Reeves' room. He found it yesterday afternoon on the railway line; Brotherhood must have dropped it when— he fell. So of course Reeves brought it back here, and it was standing up against his chair last night. There was nobody sitting there."

"But hang it all, I swear I heard somebody breathing."

"You did. That was just bad luck. The fact is, Reeves and I were fooling about inside that secret passage, and saw you come in. And the breathing was done by Reeves, off."

"Good Lord! Why didn't you tell me?"

"Well, you didn't give us much chance, did you, going and locking yourself up in your room like that? And then this morning Reeves 'phoned you up from the steward's office to tell you the news."

"What news?"

"That the mystery about Brotherhood's murder was solved."

"Oh, yes—Davenant did it, didn't he? They were telling me about it at the station."

"Well, you see, Reeves must have started by saying 'About Brotherhood,' or something like that. And then, like a fool, you dropped the tube and legged it for London."

"Well, upon my word! Do you know, Gordon, now I come to think of it, I don't mind if I do."

CHAPTER XXIV

GORDON OFFERS THE CONSOLATION OF PHILOSOPHY[1]

GORDON fell into Reeves' other arm-chair and shouted with laughter. Nothing could be more disagreeable to nerves already jangled. Reeves almost shook him into position, demanding explanations.

"It's all right," he said at last. "You get all the luck, Reeves. Marryatt wasn't listening at the other end of the metaphone. And all the time you were talking through it, it was just a soliloquy."

"Thank God for that! But how did you explain it all? What did you tell him?"

"Oh, I just told him the truth—part of the truth. And you must really get out of that habit of wheezing, because it was your wheezing behind the secret panel that made Marryatt think it was Brotherhood's ghost sitting in your room last night!"

"You mean that's what frightened Marryatt? Why did he run away this morning, then?"

"He thought it was Brotherhood telephoning to him. Lord, what a day!"

"And you've explained everything to him?"

[1] To the Reader—This chapter may be omitted if the book be thought too long.

"Yes, I've explained it all; I'd have explained it yesterday, if you'd let me."

"Come now, don't try and persuade me you didn't think yourself that Marryatt was guilty?"

"Guilty of murder? Not for a single, solitary moment. I did think there was something wrong with him—so there was, he was hag-ridden with nightmare about Brotherhood. But I never agreed with you about Marryatt being a murderer, and, to do me justice, I never said so."

"That's all very well, but you never showed me where I was wrong in my interpretation of the whole thing."

"I know; it was no good showing you where you were wrong, because you were so confoundedly ingenious at devising fresh explanations. Honestly, I did put one or two difficulties to you, but in a second you'd persuaded yourself to believe that they were no difficulties at all. And of course there were heaps more."

"Such as?"

"Well, you persisted in regarding the whole thing as a deliberate, carefully planned murder. But if you come to think of it, the circumstances that favoured the murder were just the sort of circumstances that couldn't have been foreseen. How could a man like Marryatt know that Brotherhood was due to go bankrupt? He knows no more about the City than you do. And the fog—look how the fog played up all through! How was Marryatt to know there was going to be a fog on the very day on which his attempt would be made? Yet, without a fog, the attempt would have been perfectly desperate."

"Yes, I suppose that's true."

"And it wasn't merely the general setting, it was the details. How could Marryatt know that the train would be held up by signals just there? How could he tell that Brotherhood would get into the part of the train which hadn't got a corridor, and that he would get into an empty carriage? What would he have been able to do, if Brotherhood had happened to come back as he always did—did, in fact, come back on Tuesday—in a crowded train like the 3.47? How could he be certain that nobody had seen Brotherhood get into the three o'clock? That nobody had noticed him at Weighford? Alternately, don't you see, you make your man take the most superhumanly cunning precautions, and then trust to blind chance. But those are all objections of detail. I didn't mention them because, as I say, you'd have found some sort of answer for each. My real objection was much deeper."

"Well, why didn't you tell me about *that?*"

"Because you wouldn't have begun to understand it. It's concerned, you see, with people, not with things. It's simply that Davenant is the kind of person who would kill a man, and Marryatt isn't."

"You mean because Marryatt's a parson? But, dash it all, Davenant goes to church."

"Davenant goes to church, but he isn't the sort of

person who goes to church. With Protestants, I mean, it's ordinarily safe to assume that if people do go to church they are of a church-going type; they belong to the 'unco' guid.' That isn't a safe assumption to make about Catholics; they seem to go to church whether they're 'unco' guid' or not. I don't mean that Davenant's a stage villain, but he's just an ordinary sort of person, and he's got red blood in him, whereas Marryatt hasn't— I hope it's not unkind to say so. He wouldn't kill a man; you may almost say he couldn't."

"Couldn't morally, you mean, or couldn't physically?"

"I don't mean either. 'Couldn't psychically' would be nearer the mark. For one thing, Davenant's fought in the war, and killed people, I expect—he was a bombing officer, wasn't he? Well, you know, I think to most people that makes an enormous difference. I suppose that's why there's generally a 'crime-wave' after wars—part of the reason, anyhow. People have got accustomed to killing, and it isn't easy to murder people till you've done that."

"And Marryatt, you mean, really couldn't kill a man?"

"Physically he could—he's rather strong. Morally he could—morally any of us could do anything. Or so they taught us when we were small. But there's a third difficulty you've got to get over, if you want to murder people; a sort of nervous repugnance to the job. I don't say that if Marryatt went to the bad, he mightn't screw himself up to the point of shoving poison into somebody's tea. But he couldn't kill a man with his hands."

"I know; it doesn't sound probable. And yet, I suppose a person with a fixed idea isn't much different from a madman, is he? And my argument was that Marryatt had a sort of fixed idea about religion."

"Yes; but, don't you see, he hasn't. Marryatt's a very good chap, and he thinks all the doctrines he preaches are more probable than not, but his religion doesn't sweep him off his feet: the man who denies it doesn't seem to him something less than human. That was another reason against your theory. Psychologically, Marryatt hasn't got the apparatus to do what you thought he did. Morally, he hasn't got the motive to act as you thought he did."

"Well, I seem to have made a pretty good ass of myself all round. I wonder if anybody in the world has ever been so led astray by a theory?"

"Anybody ever? Why, my dear Reeves, you're in exactly the same position there as about three-quarters of the modern world: they are all led astray by theories. Only you were at least led astray by your own theory, not by one you'd borrowed at second-hand."

"What, you mean scientific theories in medicine and so on? Taking the doctors' word for it that it's a good thing to be vaccinated, and that kind of thing?"

"No, hang it all, it would be unfair to complain of that. It's better for the doctors to have a false theory than no theory at all. They make mistakes, but sooner or later they find out they were wrong. It's bad luck on all the people who happen to have died from getting the wrong treatment, but still, we did our best. No, I don't mean the guess-work by which we live from day to day, and which is necessary to living: I mean the theories learned people propound to us about the past, about the meaning of human history."

"Darwin, and all that?"

"No, not exactly. I grant you that does illustrate my point. Evolution is only a theory, and the relationship of the monkey to the man not even a plausible theory; and yet they have gone on so long without being positively disproved that everybody talks as if they were proved. The scientist still treats evolution as a theory, the educationalist treats it as a fact. There's a curious sort of statute of limitations in the learned world which makes it impossible to call a man a liar if he has gone on lying successfully for fifty years. But, after all, there's something to be said for the Evolutionists. They did set out to explain a real problem, why there should be more than one kind of thing in the world; and they don't even profess to have explained it. The theorizers I mean are people who create problems where none exist—as you did, Reeves, when you insisted on regarding it as an open question who murdered Brotherhood. They are people who trust circumstantial evidence in the face of all common human probability, as you did, Reeves, when you wanted to convict a chump like Marryatt of murder on the strength of a chain of silly coincidences."

"All this comes out of your diary, I suppose?"

"No, I haven't written it up yet. I'm going to write it up, about half an hour from now, that's why you're getting all this thrown at you. You see, when I think of you talking through that metaphone, it strikes me as a splendid allegory of the whole historical method in criticism—or rather, that abuse of the historical method which commonly usurps the title. The man who has theories about history is usually just that—a man talking down the metaphone, making a series of false statements to a person who isn't there, and defying him to disprove them."

"Gordon, I believe you're going to solve the problem of my vocation. I've always hankered after being an amateur detective, but it seems to me the job is less attractive than I supposed—facts will keep coming in. But, by your way of it, it sounds as if I might be a success in one of the learned professions."

"Certainly. Be an anthropologist, Reeves. Fish up a lot of facts, alleged on very doubtful authority, about primitive man—his marriage ceremonies, his burial customs, his system of land tenure. Look at the whole mass of facts squint-eyed until you can see a theory in it. Embrace the theory; trot out all the facts which support your theory; write a long appendix on all the facts which contradict your theory, showing them to be insignificant or irrelevant (you'd do that all right) and there you are. You'll do quite as good anthropological research as—

—"

"Is there money in it?"

"I thought you were all right for money. No, if you're out for that, I should take to psycho-analysis. The system's the same, generally speaking, only instead of dealing with primitive man, whom you can disregard because he isn't there, you are dealing with a living man, who will probably tell you that you are a liar. Then you tell him that he is losing his temper, which is the sign of a strong inhibition somewhere, and that's just what you were saying all along. The beauty of psycho-analysis is that it's all 'Heads-I-win-tails-you-lose.' In medicine, your diagnosis of fever is a trifle disconcerted if the patient's temperature is sub-normal. In psychoanalysis you say, 'Ah, that just proves what I was saying.' "

"It seems to me that I have been neglecting all these openings for our young men."

"Well, I don't know, the psycho-business is getting a bit over-crowded nowadays. But there are still plenty of openings in the historical line. You can read what theories you like into history, as long as you are careful to neglect human probabilities, and take your evidence entirely from a selection of external facts. There is danger in it, of course; any day some fool may dig up a great chunk of Livy, and all your theories go wrong. Still, the obvious remedy for that is to say that Livy was lying on purpose, leaving false clues about deliberately, like Marryatt, you know, on the railway line. All documents, you see, which don't happen to support your point of view, thereby give themselves away as being late and untrustworthy."

"But I don't think I know any history much."

"That doesn't matter; it's quite easy to read your stuff up if you confine yourself to a particular period or a particular kind of history. For the beginner, Church history may be confidently recommended. Public interest in the subject is so small that it is very unlikely any one will take the trouble to contradict you. If the worst comes to the worst, you can always fall back upon literary criticism, and there you are on perfectly safe ground. A man with a documentary hypothesis can defy the rudest assaults of common sense."

"How does one do that, exactly?"

"You have to start out by saying, 'This document consists of three parts. One part is genuine, one part is spurious, the third part is faked evidence put in to make the spurious stuff look as if it was genuine!' Then, you see, you are on velvet. You reject altogether the parts of the document which you don't like. Then you take the remaining part, and find that it still contains a certain sort of dross—evidence which still conflicts with your theory. That dross you purge away by calling it a deliberate fake. The watch says 4.54—that is proof positive that, in the first place, the murder took place at 3.54, and, in the second place, the murderer tried to pretend it didn't. You see the idea? Now, the more of that business you do, the more ingenious your theory becomes, and the more ingenious your theory becomes, the more easily will people accept it as true. Half the statements which we regard as facts in history and criticism are statements made by critics, which are so ingenious that nobody has the heart to doubt them. And so the silly old world goes on. What if our forefathers are misjudged? We keep our mouths, not our ears, to the metaphone, and the honourable gentlemen get no opportunity to reply: and it doesn't matter much to them, because, like sensible people, they've dropped their end of the tube, and left us to talk into empty air."

"Do you know, Gordon, I believe you talk an awful lot of rot."

"I know. But it isn't all rot. Well, what *are* you proposing to do?"

"I am proposing to devote myself in future to the Game—the Game, the whole Game, and nothing but the Game."

CHAPTER XXV

THE DULL FACTS

THE DORMY-HOUSE,
PASTON OATVILE,
BINVER

MY DEAR GORDON,

Reeves has just been in to inform me that Davenant has been hung. A laughable misconception, of course; he has not been hung, he has been hanged.

I write as you asked me to write, to supply what information I can about the actual course of events in connection with what is locally called the Links Mystery. I have put it together with some difficulty; part of it, of course, came out at the trial; part I had from Miss Rendall-Smith, part from the priest at Paston Bridge, upon whom I called specially for the purpose. A not unintelligent man, who seemed to me to know more about the neighbourhood and the people who live here than Marryatt will ever know. He was, of course, debarred by professional scruples from telling me one or two things about which my curiosity prompted me to ask, but he did not appear to be unduly distressed about Davenant. "Depend upon it, Mr. Carmichael," he said, "there's others do worse and never get found out. A nice, clean death he'll make of it. Goes to Communion every morning, you know—an example to all of us." I told him, of course, that I was not narrow-minded, and could see good in all religions.

Well, the outlines of the thing seem to have been very simple indeed. Davenant saw that Brotherhood meant to persecute the lady because of the money, and determined to try and dissuade him. Brotherhood was just leaving the office when Davenant reached it; Davenant hailed a taxi, and followed him. Brotherhood did not go straight to the station; he went to a flat somewhere out Chelsea way—no doubt this was where he used to spend his weekends. No doubt he had decided that this double life must come to an end, now that it was necessary for him to live on his wife's money, and therefore wanted to collect all his personal effects. He came out in about ten minutes' time, cramming an old-fashioned watch into his waistcoat pocket—presumably, in the hurry of the moment, he wound up this watch, which had been left about in the flat, mistiming it by an hour. With the help of the taximan he managed to get an enormous trunk on to the cab and then set out for the station: He was nipping pretty freely from a flask in his pocket. Davenant shadowed him all the way at a distance: he could not have kept up with him if he had not heard his orders to the taxi-driver.

When he got to the station, Brotherhood bought a third-class ticket, and crammed it in his waistcoat pocket. The purpose of this appeared when he was having his trunk labelled—it was cheaper than paying excess luggage. He had his season-ticket in his great-coat pocket. By the way, why did we not question ourselves more over the singular fact that Brotherhood's body was found without umbrella or great-coat, on such an inclement day? He got into a first-class carriage, already occupied; and Davenant, seeing that there was no chance of a personal interview, travelled third himself, always hoping than something would turn up.

At Paston Oatvile something did turn up— Brotherhood got out of the train decidedly the worse for drink. Davenant, it is clear, had up to this time no sinister intentions, for he talked to one of the porters when he alighted, and then went up to Brotherhood and hailed him as an acquaintance. Brotherhood was far too muzzy to be afraid of him; he hailed him as good old Davenant, and suggested that they should have a drink between trains at the inn opposite the station. Davenant knew that drinks were not served at that hour, but he accompanied him willingly enough; they wasted a little time trying the door, and then saw the train for Paston Whitchurch steaming out of the station. You will observe that Brotherhood was by now artificially deprived of his luggage. His box went on to Binver, so did his great-coat (with the season-ticket in it) which he had thrown into the 4.50 from the platform. Both were afterwards recovered by the police, but were of little use to them.

Had Brotherhood been sober, he would have gone back to the station, no doubt, so as to telegraph to Binver about his things. As it was, he willingly fell in with Davenant's suggestion that they should walk across to Paston Whitchurch by the field path, crossing the valley by the railway viaduct. They walked, then, through the fog, not much behind the train; perhaps Davenant may even have suggested the possibility of overtaking it if it were held up by the signals. They did not, in fact, overtake it. Davenant began to commiserate with Brotherhood upon his bankruptcy, at which Brotherhood became extremely cheerful, and explained that he had a wife, a deuced fine woman, who had got a lot of his money in her own name, and he was going back to her. Davenant expostulated, threatened, implored; nothing would disturb the drunkard's irritating good temper. Finally, Brotherhood became lyrical over the charms of his wife just as they began to cross the viaduct. It was too much for Davenant; in a fit of disgusted rage, he turned and threw his gross companion over the edge of the slope. There was one startled cry, and then nothing but silence and the fog.

Up to that moment Davenant had no plans; he had not thought of murder even as a contingency. It is true, he had to confess to having sent the cipher warning: but this, he insisted, had been a mere threat; he was anxious to prevent Brotherhood doing anything before he could have a talk with him. By the way, Brotherhood was at home the week-end before his death, contrary to his usual custom. Mrs. Bramston does not abide our question, otherwise we might have elicited the fact from her. Davenant travelled up in the same train with him, and saw him beginning Momerie's *Immortality*—that was on the Monday morning; he bought a copy himself at the bookstall and sent the cipher to him, thinking he would probably be still reading the same book the next day. The whole idea of the cipher, he says, was a mere foolish whim on his part.

He now found himself in urgent need of plans. He did not know whether his victim was dead: yet it would be risky to go right down into the valley, and perhaps find that a corpse had already been discovered. He determined to go and hide until he got more news about this. Meanwhile, the fog prevented him from seeing whether he had made a clean job of it. He searched a little, and found Brotherhood's hat a little way down the slope; that meant that he had not fallen sheer—he might have left his stick behind too as he fell. This, however, Davenant could not see in the fog. He took the hat to the point at which the viaduct railing began; and a little further, secure that this, at any rate, would fall clear. He then measured a few yards back, and dropped a golf-ball to mark the spot. He thought, you see, that he might want to go back there in better weather and look for the stick. Then he turned back along the line and took the path down to the dormy-house. The fog was beginning to lift, but he met nobody. He knew the secret passage from his boyhood, and thanked his stars that he had never mentioned its existence to any one in the Club. He had a confederate, of course, among the Club servants—Miss Rendall-Smith says she thinks it was an old servant of his family's; and this man, whose name has never appeared, helped him to hide in the passage and brought him, by arrangement with Sullivan, the necessities of living.

It was from our own conversation—a singular thought!—that he got most of his news. His confinement, by the way, was not very irksome, since he knew the habits of the members so well. He used to shave in the Club washing-room, for example; and got pickings from the food that went down to the kitchen. More than once, when he knew there was no danger of interruption, he came out into the billiard-room and played a game, right against left. He could keep in touch with all that went on, and it was his intention, I gather, to come out of his hiding-place in any case on the Saturday afternoon, play a round in the evening, and go back to the Hatcheries that night as if nothing had happened. That was, of course, when the verdict of suicide at the inquest made it seem as if he was free from all suspicion.

But our proceedings bothered him badly. Especially

the photograph; he guessed from our talk that it must be Miss Rendall-Smith's, and knew that it was likely to direct attention to her. He did not hope to steal it, because the loss would be too obvious, but he could not resist putting his arm through the sliding panel while we were playing Bridge and just taking a look at it. He had himself a photograph of Miss Rendall-Smith in his pocket, taken at the same sitting: when he first heard us talking about photographs, he pulled this out to make sure he had not lost it; and when he had the second photograph in his hands he switched on his electric torch for an instant (a risky thing to do) and compared them. Then, in the dark, he put back the wrong one by mistake.

Why he was so anxious to get back the copy of the cipher, he did not explain. I fancy when he first contemplated the idea he imagined that we had the original; and to that, as we shall see, he did attach importance. But he did not think he took much risk when he purloined the cipher and put it back again on finding it useless, or when he came out at night to see what souvenirs of Brotherhood Reeves had got. I think he was afraid of some fresh clue which might inculpate Miss Rendall-Smith; and he imagined, of course, that the watch at the door was the only thing he had to be frightened of.

It was only next morning that he found some of my chewing gum on his trousers, and guessed that a trap had been laid for him. As soon as he heard our movements upstairs he stepped out into the billiard-room, and got his confederate to hide him somewhere in the servants' quarters. It was when news was brought to him that the police were investigating the cellar entrance that he really took alarm, and decided to bolt for it. Even then he kept his head, and if Reeves had been a little less close on his trail he would have come back quietly to Paston Whitchurch on that slow train, and it would have been very difficult to incriminate him. As it was, it was only a stiff door-handle that gave him away.

It was Miss Rendall-Smith who explained to me the mysterious writing on the back of the cipher. The words were, of course, explained by what was written on the other half-sheet before the sheet was torn in two. Miss Rendall-Smith showed me the full text of the thing, and I confess that at first it meant nothing to me; you, no doubt, would have taken the point with more readiness. Here it is, anyhow.

S O
C R
H a S   socks
I n tE   rest
S heC   hem
M a T   tins.

It appears that this forms an acrostic, and is connected with some kind of competition in the weekly papers. The two first words have not been successfully identified, the four last have. All we saw on our half-sheet was the non-significant termination of the last four words. I took it to Lees-Jones—you remember Lees-Jones, our Acrostic expert?—and he said it would have been very difficult to reconstruct the original acrostic from these indications. Your critical faculty will not fail to be delighted by the mistake we made in reading "rest" as "vest," simply because it came next to the word "socks," which set up a train of mental association.

It appears that Davenant used to toy with this peculiar sport, and Miss Rendall-Smith occasionally helped him. On the Sunday before the murder she sent him the answer, as far as she could decipher it, on a full sheet of note-paper, and he tore off half of this when he wanted to write the cipher message to Brotherhood. The writing was Miss Rendall-Smith's own, and I fancy it was purely through that, with the help of the Post Office, that the police got on her track.

The sleeper-coupon was the most misleading clue of all. It appears certain that Brotherhood himself did not know of his impending bankruptcy when he applied for it, and merely intended a business visit to Glasgow; indeed, he was expected there. The correction was quite a genuine one, necessitated by an error on the part of the clerk. And that, I think, finishes the list of enigmas. It was, of course, Miss Rendall-Smith who sent the other wreath. And it was Marryatt (I found out by tactful questioning) who took the copy of Momerie from Reeves' shelves—he was looking for material for his evening sermon.

The only problem that remains to me is this— Do we really know in full the part which Miss Rendall-Smith plays in the story? Davenant's excessive anxiety to keep her out of the whole business looks to me, I confess, suspicious. But I know how you distrust theories; and perhaps since Davenant was content to die in silence it would be ungenerous to probe further. The police, certainly, have made no attempt to do so. Reeves has never called on Miss R.-S., or heard from her.

Reeves himself, meanwhile, is entirely changed for the better. He has forsworn detective work, and succeeded in doing the ninth in four. The other day I actually heard him start a sentence with the words "When I was a limpet in the War Office," so I think there is hope for him yet. I call him "Mordaunt Reeves, the Converted Detective."

I hope you will excuse my typewriting this letter; its inordinate length must be my apology. I hope we shall see you here again before long, and have less stirring times together. My wife wishes to be remembered to you very kindly; her rheumatism has almost disappeared.

Yours sincerely,
WILLIAM CARMICHAEL